"What in the hell happened?"

"I—you grabbed me," she said shakily.

"That's not what I meant and you damned well know it." The rough harshness in his deep voice sharpened into a lethal, cutting edge. "Who's been giving you lessons?"

"Lessons?"

"You sure as hell didn't kiss me like that the last time around. Do you get your kicks from blowing hot one moment and cool the next? That's a dangerous game, Olivia. I hope you're prepared for the consequences."

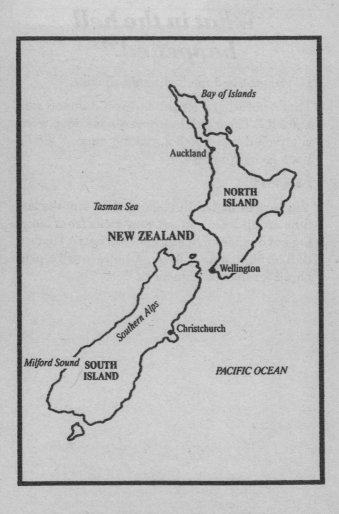

SUSAN NAPIER

Winter of Dreams

Harlequin Books

TORONTO • NEW YORK • LONDON
AMSTERDAM • PARIS • SYDNEY • HAMBURG
STOCKHOLM • ATHENS • TOKYO • MILAN
MADRID • WARSAW • BUDAPEST • AUCKLAND

Harlequin Presents first edition October 1993
ISBN 0-373-11595-4

Original hardcover edition published in 1992
by Mills & Boon Limited

WINTER OF DREAMS

Printed in U.S.A.

CHAPTER ONE

'You look absolutely terrible!'

Olivia Marlow glared blearily at her twin, sitting cheerfully at the end of the bed, a picture of blooming health.

'Thanks, Roz, that makes me feel a load better.'

The sarcasm was blithely ignored. 'No, really, you look *dire.*'

Although they weren't identical twins Olivia and Rosalind were similar enough to have had great fun confusing people during their growing years. However, as they progressed through their early twenties, Roz's career as a stage and television actress had blossomed, and she had acquired all the requisite gloss of her profession. Even in her tatty rehearsal gear of worn jeans and a threadbare sweater Roz managed to look classy. In the same clothes Olivia would have looked merely scruffy. But then, actresses were expected to be glamorous and painters to be scruffy. They were both in their own way just living up to the world's expectations...

'I thought the doctor had given you a clean bill.'

'He has.' Olivia had wanted so badly to get back to her solitary studio that she had virtually hounded the family doctor until he agreed that she was fit enough to look after herself. It wasn't that conditions were cramped in her parents' town house, or that they made her feel unwanted. Quite the reverse. It was their tacit understanding and loving concern that was so hard to take. As a playwright Michael Marlow was too familiar with the effects of an artistic block not to recognise it in others and her actress mother had already turned down one plum role to care for her convalescing daughter. As long as her parents knew that she wasn't working they would worry and her mother would feel it necessary to indulge her maternal guilt by sacrificing her own career. At least tucked away here, in her loft on top of an inner-city Auckland warehouse, she could pretend that she was picking up the threads of her artistic life.

'Then why do you look so rotten?'

Olivia's irritation overrode her apathy. 'Roz, if you came here to cheer me up, your bedside manner leaves a lot to be desired.'

Rosalind only grinned, her green eyes smug with secrets. The sophisticate was superseded by a gamine, the newly short-cropped hair making her look like a red-headed elf. 'Look, why don't you get up while I make breakfast and I'll tell you something that will do you more good than any amount of oozing sympathy?'

It was past time Olivia should have been getting up, but sleep was a useful tool for procrastination. Reluctantly Olivia pushed down the bedclothes and climbed out of the high narrow bed which took up one corner of the huge loft, shivering slightly as her bare feet hit the cool polished floorboards. She rifled through the clothes hanging on a portable rail, grateful that her head no longer spun when she moved, although the lethargy that had dogged her for months still dragged at her limbs. Her recovery would be much slower than normal, the doctor had advised her sternly, since she had put off seeking professional help until she had literally collapsed.

'Just coffee will do. I'm not very hungry,' she said as her sister began to bustle in the kitchen alcove on the other side of the huge square room. Weak autumn sunlight slanted in through the huge cantilevered windows, picking out the rich colours in the hand-woven rugs scattered around the floor and sculpting patterns across the uneven plaster of the rough-cast walls. Olivia had felt little need for anything more than the most basic articles of furniture in her living-cum-work space. Her lovingly selected art collection provided the substance of the room.

'The doctor said you have to re-build your stamina, you're as thin as a rake,' Roz said, her powerful voice projecting effortlessly across the high-ceilinged room.

'So are you,' Olivia pointed out, pulling on thick pink fluorescent socks under her baggy black tracksuit, taming her long red hair into a careless pony-tail as she joined her sister.

'Yes, but *I'm* working out for five hours a day.' Roz was currently starring on stage in a vigorous musical production which had made Olivia sweat just to watch. 'What you see is all finely tuned muscle. Right now you're just skin and bone. All that lovely fatty insulation has melted away.'

It was a family joke. The few ounces' difference in their low birth weight had led to Olivia being referred to as 'the fat one'. She had never been overweight but she had definitely had more curves than her sister, a fact Roz teasingly bemoaned.

Olivia sighed and took a bite of the toast that was plonked in front of her. It tasted like cardboard. Her taste-buds had failed her quite as spectacularly as her artistic inspiration, one reason she had found it so difficult to regain weight after her long illness.

Roz looked around the studio and asked casually, 'Done any work lately?'

Olivia shrugged, the familiar hunted feeling closing in on her. Her art school training, the year in Paris and the subsequent two years working in Spain and New York with Diego had all been directed towards preparing her for artistic success, not failure. Even the belated discovery that there was a medical reason for what she had thought was a complete emotional and artistic burn-out had not relieved her anxieties. Previously always in good health, although more by default than by any positive efforts on her own behalf, Olivia had found glandular fever a particularly depressing and restrictive illness. On the rare occasions over the past few months when she *had* felt the impulse to work, she had found that she lacked the energy to carry it through. Her single most important source of inspiration had dried up and she was sometimes afraid that she would never get her motivation back.

In the last three months she had not completed a single work. For a painter as vital and as prolific as Olivia had been that was equivalent to a lifetime. The six Marlow children had all been expected to support themselves once they were qualified in their fields and Olivia had managed, with some juggling, to live solely from her art. Thanks to a trust fund which Olivia had inherited when she had turned twenty-five the previous year, she would never have to worry about starving in the street, but she was guiltily aware that the easy availability of money was yet another creeping disincentive to work...no doubt the reason why her parents had decided that none of the children should receive his or her inheritance until each had developed his or her independence and, hopefully, the maturity to handle wealth.

'Well, forget everything else,' Roz cut across her brooding thoughts. 'Guess what three artists made the short-list for the Pendragon commission?'

'This is supposed to cheer me up?' asked Olivia incredulously.

'Guess?' her twin insisted stubbornly.

'Steven Foscoe,' said Olivia glumly. She didn't know him personally but she had seen, admired, and even envied some of his works. His workings in metal were often interpreted as aggressive, masculine statements about power and control and their size and scope would no doubt be well suited to the images evoked by the Pendragon Corporation with its aggressive domination of the New Zealand agricultural industry. Like the dragon on its logo, the company had crushed and consumed many a vulnerable prey. However, in the last few years the ageing figurehead of the company, Alun Pendragon, had revealed sudden largesse. He had been generous in his sponsorship of charities, sports events and the performing arts, and several months ago had announced plans for the single most expensive art commission in New Zealand. Artists were invited to apply for the opportunity to produce not only a series of theme works for the foyer of the new Pendragon Corporation headquarters under construction in Wellington, but also a major piece for the Pendragon-sponsored performing arts centre being built in Auckland. Even solidly established artists had drooled at the prospect of such prominent exposure in New Zealand's two largest cities and, for someone like Olivia, newly returned to her own country and still relatively unknown there, it was an opportunity she couldn't afford to ignore. At the time she had been working frantically on her first solo exhibition, but had succumbed to the pressure from family and friends and fired off a portfolio of ideas to the Pendragon Corporation. Of course, that was when she had still believed that she was worthy of the challenge...

'And?'

'John Ferris?'

'And?'

They were the two obvious choices. Olivia had to think about the third.

'Rachel Omer?'

'Nope.' Roz's expression of smugness increased as Olivia made one or two more half-hearted guesses. It was tough to sound interested when you just wanted to bawl your head off.

'I could sit here all day guessing but wouldn't it be easier if you just told me?' she said irritably.

'Olivia Marlow!'

'Who?'

'My God, you're even further gone than I thought!' Roz cried in frustration at her blank reaction. 'Olivia Marlow. You, you dummy! It's *you*! *You're* the third.'

Olivia went from baffled to furious to hurt within the space of a heartbeat. 'That's not funny, Roz,' she said shakily, her eyes suddenly stinging.

Roz, too, was hurt. 'Livvy, I wouldn't joke about something as important as this. Look, I have the letter right here.' She dug among the crumpled scripts and odd bits of clothing and make-up stuffed into her cavernous black leather bag.

Olivia shook her head, shocked by her twin's callousness. 'Stop it, Roz. How can I be on a short-list when I didn't even attend the panel?'

She had made the first cut-off, had been invited to spend the weekend at Alun Pendragon's home on the shores of Lake Taupo in the central North Island to make an informal presentation of her ideas to the Corporation and to talk about herself and show examples of her current work. But by that time she had been firmly in the numbing grip of her depressive illness, certain that her every endeavour was doomed to failure and unwilling to risk another public humiliation.

'Look.' Roz finally found what she was looking for and thrust an envelope at her sister. 'Go on, read it!'

Olivia had to blink hard before the writing came into focus. Most of the signature was indistinguishable but there was certainly a dragon in there somewhere and the letter-head was unarguably the Corporation's. 'But...this is impossible!' she whispered. 'There has to be some mistake. They've got me mixed up with someone else!'

Each of the artists on the short-list was to embark on a minor commission as the final stage of the selection process, the letter stated concisely. Hers was a portrait of Alun Pendragon, as discussed during her stay at Lake Taupo, to be executed at his home at a date convenient for both.

'This is ridiculous,' she said hoarsely. 'I never stayed there, this is all a ghastly mistake... and look, this isn't even my ad-dress...' Her protest broke up on the last word as she recognised the street name and number on the envelope. Roz's flat. She lowered the letter accusingly.

'I never sent that letter of refusal you gave me to post,' Roz confessed flatly, eyeing her sister's pale face cautiously.

Olivia was totally bewildered. 'But that doesn't explain *this*. You can't tell me they'd choose me over all the others when I didn't even bother to turn up to talk about my ideas——' A grim laugh. 'Such as they were.'

'They were great! And you did.'

'Did what?'

'Turn up.'

Olivia's head was suddenly aching again. She had been extremely ill, yes, but she didn't think that she had been so totally out of it that she could have sleep-walked to Taupo and back!

'Not only did you meet them but you impressed them mightily, especially the old guy.'

'Old guy?' said Olivia muzzily. This was a simple misunderstanding, she told herself desperately. Roz couldn't *really* be saying what Olivia *thought* she was saying.

'The dragon himself, Alun Pendragon. He was a tough nut but they're the only ones worth cracking. You just have to stand up to him, let him know you're not overawed by all his fire-breathing...'

'Roz...' Olivia's voice was a raw croak '...you couldn't have—you didn't—you *wouldn't* have...?'

'Could, did, would!' Roz said starkly, becoming defensive as Olivia closed her horrified eyes. 'Well, someone had to do *something*, Liv. I thought your ideas were terrific—and obviously so did everyone else!' Roz snatched the letter up and shook it under her sister's outraged nose.

'You took it upon yourself to make a major decision about my life without my knowledge or consent?' Olivia burst out furiously, still unwilling to believe it. 'You actually went *down* there and pretended *you* were *me*?'

'Only for the weekend,' said Roz modestly. 'Well, only a day and a half really. No one suspected a thing——'

'But they certainly would if they ever met the *real* me,' Olivia pointed out savagely. 'We might be twins but we're two totally different people——'

'One of whom is an award-winning actress!' asserted Roz unblushingly. 'Darling, I've trained for *years* to project myself into other people's personalities. Believe me, you've got nothing to worry about!'

Olivia had the feeling her worries were only beginning. Just thinking about what Roz had risked sent her into a cold sweat. 'We don't even look alike any more. What on earth made you think we could pull it off?'

'Have you looked at yourself in the mirror lately?'

Olivia scowled. She knew how dreadful she looked; she didn't need Roz, or mirrors, to tell her.

Rosalind sighed. She dived back into her bag and produced a double-sided magnifying mirror. She trotted round the table and set it in front of Olivia, then leaned over her shoulder so that their reflections appeared as a double image. Olivia stared, startled at what she saw. Allowing for the fact that Roz was wearing make-up and she wasn't, their faces looked more similar than they had since they had entered their terrible teens. Before her illness Olivia's face had been as softly rounded as the rest of her, making her eyes and mouth seem smaller, the whole adding up to a wholesome prettiness. Now she had cheekbones as haughty as her sister's, and cheeks that needed no shading to look fashionably hollow. Her eyes looked more prominent in the ruthlessly refined oval of her skull and her mouth proportionately larger. Fragility and strength, sameness and difference, the dichotomy within and between each face made Olivia's lethargic imagination stir. The most striking superficial difference was that Roz dyed her eyebrows and lashes dark brown, and, of course——

'Your eyes...?' Olivia's eyes were a soft, misty colour, like a rain-washed sea. Roz's were a dramatic bottle-green.

'Contact lenses.'

'And your hair?' For most of their lives Olivia had worn hers cropped, as Roz's was now, but during the last wretched year, starting with that humiliatingly abortive love-affair in New York, Olivia had been as haphazard about hair-care as about her general health. Now it was below her shoulders, thick and straight and as undisciplined as the rest of her.

'I wore my wig.' Roz had let go her crowning glory reluctantly, only because it was necessary for a film part, but had then discovered that she liked the freedom of the new style, combined with the versatility of her re-cycled locks.

That still left one burning question. 'For God's sake, Roz, *why*?' asked Olivia quietly.

Her sister looked her straight in the eye. 'Because I love you. Because you were sick and not thinking straight. You *needed* this commission to pick you up and shake you out of this rotten depression——'

'The doctor said I should take it easy——'

'Not this easy...lying in bed all morning. That's not like you, Liv, you're letting that bloody awful man do you in——'

'For goodness' sake, Roz, that was a year ago,' Olivia said thinly, avoiding those perceptive green eyes.

'I'm not talking about Gabriel, I'm talking about that ignorant pig of a critic——'

Olivia stiffened. Her family had stepped very delicately around the subject of her exhibition, held a few months after she arrived back in New Zealand. It was never mentioned, except in the most oblique terms. But when Roz got that bullish look of determination on her face there was no point in trying to evade a head-on discussion.

'What makes you think he's a man?' she said weakly.

'Because it was obvious he was a misogynist. He didn't just attack you as an artist, but as a woman. And in all the columns I've read since he has never been that vitriolic towards a male artist...or anyone, come to that. It was almost as if he had a personal grudge against you.'

'I thought you were boycotting that paper,' said Olivia wryly, remembering Roz's rage on her behalf when the review had been published. Fortunately, for Olivia had just wanted to wipe the whole miserable episode from her mind, the paper insisted on preserving the anonymity of the controversial critic who wrote under the byline of 'the Jester', and Roz's dagger tongue had never found its mark.

'The column is syndicated,' she added sheepishly now. 'Nearly every paper in the country runs "Jester" pieces. Just think how much crow the miserable one-eyed creep will have to eat when you get this commission...'

When, not if. Roz had a great deal more confidence than Olivia. She looked down at her hands, admitting to herself what she had never admitted to anyone else, even Roz. Why should 'the Jester' have to apologise for telling the truth...? That truth haunted her every time she picked up a paintbrush, mocking her, devouring her concentration....

...imitative, weak, unfocused, a tired rehash of old ideas...not just the simple failure of a single piece of art, but a whole body of work dedicated to amateurish mediocrity...a formerly promising young talent disastrously squandered...whatever she learned in her free-wheeling years with jetsetting Spanish surrealist Diego Martinez, it obviously had nothing to do with art...

That dig at Diego was the only comment that had provoked any spark of resistance in Olivia. Yes, Diego was boisterous, erratic, larger-than-life, almost a cardboard-cut-out caricature of the bohemian artist, but he worked as hard as he partied, his enormous talent a relentless master. He, too, would have been disgusted with her first solo exhibition in her home country, and contemptuous of any excuses. To Diego, as to Olivia, mediocrity was the only inexcusable crime.

The merciless review had exploded in her face, stripping away the last refuge of her pride. For months she had worked obsessively, groping for a new direction after the emotional fiasco with Gabriel that had caused her to flee New York. She had been quite convinced that she had found it until 'the Jester' tore the blinkers from her eyes. What she had perceived as a new direction was in fact a dead end. Using mixed media rather than paint to express herself wasn't a bold experiment in textures and materials but an attempt to cover up the failure of her inner vision. The devastating revelation of self-delusion had been the last straw that broke her fragile health, the collapse of her weakened body rescuing her from the necessity of facing up to failure.

Olivia forced away the unwanted thoughts by snapping, 'Well, that's quite impossible now, isn't it? You've compromised us both with your stupid stunt. You can't draw to save your life; how did you manage to pass yourself off as an artist?'

Roz took the insult on the chin. 'It wasn't a test, Liv. Nobody handed me a pencil and said, "Here, prove yourself." All I had to do was talk——'

'But surely there must have been some discussions that got technical——'

'I'm not a total ignoramus about art. I was in that BBC series about the Impressionists, remember? I did a lot of research about art and artists. I might not be able to paint myself but I do know how it's done. Anyway, there weren't any art experts as such there, it was just the Pendragon family and a couple of advisers. They wanted me to expand on the ideas in your portfolio and that was easy because you'd rabbitted on about them for hours whenever I came over.' As she had plunged blindly into exhaustion Olivia had talked incessantly, using words to stave off the burgeoning inner panic.

'But I was supposed to have taken a recent work——'

Roz's confidence seemed to briefly falter. 'I borrowed one or two things...'

Olivia was immediately álerted. 'What one or two things exactly? I haven't produced anything worth viewing for over a year.' There, it was out. The admission. But Roz looked uneasy rather than shocked.

'Look, you're into the final stretch. What does it matter how you got there?'

'Did it ever occur to you that I might not *want* to get that commission?'

Roz's mouth dropped open. 'Of course you want it. Why wouldn't you?'

Roz didn't know how completely Olivia's dreams had deserted her. She had never told anyone how literally she had translated her dreams into reality. Without her dreams she was rudderless, her talent beyond her control. Only once had she succeeded, almost against her will, in wrenching inspiration out of reality but that, too, had had a nightmare quality about it. Olivia froze, her eyes darting to her twin's guilty face.

'No——'

She leapt across the studio with a burst of her former energy, pushing aside the screen that divided the room off her workspace. In spite of the untidy scatter over the squat, paint-splattered Formica table and the stacks of canvases leaning against the wall there was a faint air of neglect in the north corner of the loft. Feverishly Olivia searched through the canvases. When she faced her sister again they were both pale.

'Tell me you didn't...' Olivia murmured wretchedly.

'It's the best thing you've ever done,' said Roz steadily.

'I didn't know what I was doing——' Hot shame went through Olivia as she remembered how, after reading that devastating review, she had gone slightly crazy. She had rushed around to the gallery and tried to remove all the canvases. After a humiliatingly public tantrum she had crawled back to her studio and, in a fit of painful self-loathing, had attacked the canvas as if it were a bitter enemy, slashing at it, hating it, contempt in every loaded brushstroke. *The Jester*; even the name had been a black mockery. There had been nothing amusing or entertaining about what he had done to Olivia. She had worked for a week, hardly eating or sleeping, refusing to see anyone, painting herself relentlessly into a long overdue collapse. Since then she hadn't been able to bear to look at it.

'It's disgusting...'

'Only to you, Liv. No one else could doubt your talent when they look at that painting——'

'Where is it now?' Olivia was too stricken to be angry.

'Mr Pendragon wanted to keep it for a while.'

'Oh, God...' Olivia could feel herself flushing, hating to think of someone, a stranger, peering into her mind at its most bitter. Never before had she painted from sheer unadulterated hatred and the result had been, to her mind, completely grotesque.

'You can bring it back with you when you go down to do the Pendragon's portrait——'

'I'm not going! I'll just have to write and tell them I'm still too ill to consider——'

'It's too late to pull out,' said Roz quickly. 'I've already accepted. You're expected down there this week——'

'*What?*'

'Come on, Liv, what have you got to lose? Nothing! It's not as if you've got anything else pressing to do. And portraits are your forte, you love doing them. You wait until you meet Alun Pendragon; once you see him you won't be able to stand *not* to paint him!'

Roz was a persuasive debater but Olivia was unshakeable. Apart from all the fears that had shredded her sense of adventure with their needle-sharp claws, there was the principle of the thing.

'I'll ring and say I've had a sudden relapse. It would serve you right if I made *you* clear up the mess but I guess it's a little late for you to confess without implicating me.'

Roz was suitably chastened and thus all the more astonished when she called in at the studio again before her performance that evening, groaning under the weight of a small but expensive apology in the form of an exquisite stone carving by one of Olivia's favourite sculptors, to find her twin sheepishly packing winter woollies for a visit to Taupo. With a sisterly lack of tact she taunted Olivia with her change of mind.

'So, corruption is infectious, huh? What did he do, offer you more money?'

'If you're talking about Alun Pendragon I never got to talk to him.' Olivia still bristled at the memory. 'Some snooty woman called Beverly wouldn't even put me through.'

'Beverly Kelvin.' Roz pulled a face. 'She's engaged to the old man's nephew. I'm afraid she and I didn't take to each other *at all*.'

'Well, she didn't take to me either. She as good as implied right off that the portrait was just a sop to a loser. That no one with my lack of moral fibre and dubious talent would ever be allowed to contaminate the hallowed halls of the Pendragon Corporation. Moral fibre!' While Olivia might have doubts about her own talent she was damned proud of her principles.

'Sounds like par for the course for the sly witch. Beverly specialises in a nasty brew of hints and innuendoes.'

'She implied that the only dignified thing for me to do was withdraw gracefully...'

'Oh?' Roz hid a grin at Olivia's simmering words. 'You mean she wanted you to do exactly what you rang up to do? The nerve of the woman!'

Olivia glared at her. 'It was the way she put it. Like a threat, almost.'

'That's her specialty. Desperately snobbish and bulging with repressed hostility. Fantastic character study but no doubt hell to live with.'

'If I pulled out now, she would think that it was her doing.'

'Mmm, she wouldn't be above manipulating the facts to suit herself, either,' said Roz slyly, adding fuel to a fire that lately had only been sorry ashes. 'She's a fervent John Ferris fan, you know...'

Olivia had already burnt her boats when she had slammed down the receiver on the insufferably smug Beverly Kelvin. She had accepted the challenge, now she had to find the strength to tackle it.

'Who else did you "not take to" down there?' she asked her sister darkly.

'Darling, I was on my best behaviour,' laughed Roz. 'The Pendragon is a ruthless old autocrat but he respects ambition, which I projected beautifully. He had some "yes men" with him and there was his son, and the nephew who runs the company now. Funnily enough the nephew, William, is the most like the old man, but he's a bit stuffy for my liking. He's supposed to be engaged to Beverly, but I think he's a player, if you know what I mean.' Roz raised and lowered her eyebrows lecherously a few times.

'I thought you said he was stuffy.'

'The stuffy ones are always the worst. Mind you, with a fiancée like Barracuda Beverly I don't blame him for trying to snatch a little TLC on the side...'

'What about the son?'

Roz, bossily sorting through Olivia's clothes-rack, paused and then shrugged and said lightly. 'Oh, Jordan's the other way. No time for women at all——'

'You mean he's gay?' murmured Olivia absently, unshocked by the possibility as she stroked her fingers over her twin's gift, admiring the way that Junius had given warmth and movement to the crouching figure in the cool stone.

Roz made a little choking sound. 'God, I never thought—but it would certainly explain a hell of a lot.' Her voice strengthened with a hint of malicious glee that Olivia failed to notice. 'He's never married and he has to be getting on for forty. It's an awful waste, because he's sort of gorgeous in a clod-hopping, rural kind of way. You think Hugh is big? You should see this guy!'

She imitated a bulky robotic swagger that made Olivia laugh, her image of their very large, adopted eldest brother overshadowed by this new colossus. 'Maybe woman are just too tiny and insignificant to catch his attention . . . or maybe his upbringing turned him off. I gather that old man Pendragon spent more time with his business than with his family. Jordan has four older sisters, all married now and scattered around the world and they more or less brought him up after their mother died when he was born. But you don't have to worry about Jordan, because he and his father are at daggers drawn. On top of his—er—*other* problem, Jordan's a bit of a social retard. Spends most of his time down on his farm mucking about with goats or something similarly rustic—which drives his old man crazy.'

'You discovered all this in a day and a half?' Olivia's healthy glow of anger had begun to recede, leaving her with rapidly cooling feet. 'I don't have your elephantine memory, Roz; what if——?'

'Don't worry, I explained about having been ill, so that should explain any little lapses. I never told anyone where I was going that weekend and you've been so reclusive, no one would have seen you out and about here when you were supposed to be there. It's foolproof, darling!'

Where had Olivia heard *that* before? When they were children, it had always been Roz who had been the ringleader in mischief and Olivia who somehow ended up taking the blame. But in this case fate had handed her a second chance and only a mind full of positive thoughts was going to enable her to grasp it.

A positive frame of mind was, however, sadly lacking as Olivia flew over the green fields of the central North Island. Over the roar in the cockpit of the tiny plane she couldn't hear what the pilot was shouting at her but she realised sickly that it wasn't something she wanted to hear.

She hadn't felt up to making the five-hour drive to Lake Taupo herself so she had grabbed at Roz's offer to ask one of her more respectable friends, who was flying down to a wedding in Taupo in his own small plane, to give her a lift. Having only flown in large jets before, Olivia hadn't realised how bumpy the ride would be and for the last twenty minutes her heaving stomach had been wedging itself higher and higher up her throat. Any minute now she was going to be sick and she had just been wondering where the sick-bags were in the cramped cockpit, or whether she should wind down the window and fertilise some of the pastures below, when the bumpiness suddenly increased dramatically and Jonathan Whatever-his-name-was began yelling in her ear.

She *thought* it was along the lines of, 'I think we have a problem.' At least she had stopped feeling sick. Her stomach had petrified into a solid mass.

'Plenty of places to land!' Jonathan yelled at her, grinning at her as if he didn't have both their lives poised in the balance. Perhaps he thought his grin was re-assuring. Why hadn't she noticed before that he didn't look old enough to drive a car, let alone fly a plane? 'No worries—as long as we don't prang in the drink!'

Certainly not old enough to carry off that ridiculous World-War-One-flying-ace patois!

Olivia gritted her teeth as she saw the flat silver ir-regular heart-shape that was Lake Taupo rush up at them. Then, with a clever swoop that desolidified the contents of her stomach, Jonathan banked the fragile, spluttering aircraft and to Olivia's horror landed with reckless skill in a narrow rectangular paddock bordering the road, scattering a few odd sheep in the process, and jolting to a halt on the uneven turf.

'Nearly had lamb chop for tea,' quipped the relentlessly cheerful Jonathan as one woolly laggard shot under the wing. 'We might have made it a couple more kilometres to the Pendragons's airstrip but it gets a bit hilly over there and I wasn't going to take any chances. Sounded like the fuel-line—hey, are you all right?'

Olivia, her face roughly the same shade as her eyes, was scrabbling for the door-release.

'It's OK, we're down now. Sorry if you were scared, Olivia, I was just kidding about the lake, you know; we weren't really in any danger.' Jonathan at least seemed to realise that she was in no condition to appreciate his boisterous sense of humour. 'Didn't Roz tell you I'm a pilot in the air force?'

'No, and I thought you were a comedian!' choked Olivia sarcastically, wrenching a lever as a last resort and stumbling out the door to be sick in the grass.

'God, Roz is going to kill me. Are you OK?' She opened her eyes a little later to see the gung-ho pilot looked so terrified at the thought of her sister that Olivia gave a weak smile.

'It wasn't so much your flying as my constitution,' she said. 'I'm the nervous type.' She was going to show him her bitten nails to prove it, and then remembered that Roz had given her a ruthless manicure at the same time she had dyed Olivia's lashes and brows, scolding her about her neglected hands.

'Not even for you would I cannibalise myself,' Roz had said, clipping away years of neglected cuticles. 'A trim and plain polish was a far as I was prepared to go. You'll just have to give up chewing on yourself for the duration. A disgusting habit anyway.'

Jonathan was all solicitousness now, even though she saw him look at his watch a few times, obviously nervous that he wouldn't make his wedding if he had a helpless female to look after. He radioed in his position to the

Taupo control tower and just as he was going to request some alternative transport they heard something loud approaching along the road. Jonathan ran out to flag the vehicle down while Olivia weakly unloaded her precious canvas and materials, leaving her heavier case for her knight of the air to drag out.

The pick-up wasn't the cleanest of vehicles and with her uncertain stomach Olivia chose to ride in the back with three bales of hay and a very friendly dog, while Jonathan very chivalrously joined her, letting his suit-bag keep the affable and helpful farmer company in the cab.

The trip was winding as they drew nearer the rising hills that surrounded the base of Mt Tongariro and the wind whipping past her head was painfully chilly in spite of Olivia's thick hand-knitted sweater and the matching hat that covered her ears. She must have started looking green again because Jonathan began nervously reassuring her over and over that they were nearly there when the pick-up turned into a gateway flanked by twin stone dragons that caught Olivia's jaundiced artist's eye.

The quick turn of her head to study their curious conformation was a mistake. Her stomach rebelled against the motion and as soon as the pick-up had rolled to a stop in front of the impressive cedar homestead Olivia was back observing nature in close-up, this time a beautifully tended rose-bed.

She was barely aware of someone else joining the concerned farmer and anxiously patient Jonathan; all she knew was that when her stomach was vilely empty and she was aware enough to care about her surroundings the other two had gone, and the only person left to witness the humiliation of her ignominious arrival was a man she had hoped never to see again in all her born days.

'*You*! Oh, God, no... you're *all* I need!'

Her groan was uttered with such heartfelt disgust that the big, calloused hand on the back of her neck tightened menacingly, a tawny gold sheen of anger glazing across the man's narrowed blue eyes until he reined it in.

'You're right about that, Olivia.' His voice was every bit as deep and velvety as she remembered, even flattened by the heavily sardonic tone.

Jordan Pendragon rose to his considerable height and stared down at the huddled lump of misery at his feet. 'I wondered how long it was going to take you to admit it. Now you have, maybe we can stop playing games with each other!'

CHAPTER TWO

OLIVIA heard the words but they made no sense.

'Games? I'm not playing games...' She didn't dare move in case her stomach protested again. She eased back on the cold grass and squinted up at the man. The sun was behind him, causing the shaggy blond hair to light up like a nimbus around his head. No, not blond. Gold. The artist in her had made a subconscious note of the unusually intense colour the first time they had met. From this angle he looked extremely tall, and massively broad in a pale sweater and cream jeans. Unfortunately she knew that it wasn't just an optical illusion, a flattering trick of the light. If she got to her feet he would still dwarf her five-foot-ten frame. He was a big man. Big and... pushy.

He sank down again on his haunches and her abdomen tensed. His powerful arms hung forward over his splayed knees, his bulging thighs forming an open V directly in front of her, a distracting masculine threat to her wandering attention.

'I'm going to be sick again,' she said, hoping to get him to back off, since there was no prospect of her being able to force a physical show-down.

'No, you're not. What's the matter, Olivia, too embarrassed to face me?'

She gritted her teeth and forced herself to meet his gaze, cringing inside at the impact. 'Why should I be?'

'You tell me.' His eyes were blue but they weren't both the same shade and they made his square, brutally rugged face look lopsided, uneven.

'Are you following me?' she demanded, annoyed by his cryptic utterances.

'You're the one throwing out the lures, Kitten. What happened up there—did you make a pass at the pretty fly-boy in mid-air? He certainly took off from here like a guilty bat out of hell.'

'He had a wedding to go to.' Olivia scooted backwards and got up, infuriated by the man's mocking allegations. OK, so she had been deliberately rude and insulting to him last time he had tried to help, but he must have known she was distraught. She swayed, flinching as he put out a huge hand, but he was just plucking a piece of hay from her sleeve.

'Via a roll in the hay?'

'Look, I don't know what you're implying——'

His thick blond eyebrows shot up, his mouth, a thin slash in the rugged jaw, tightening. 'I never thought you were stupid, Olivia. I just wondered whether you come on to every man the way you came on to me...'

Olivia was trying, with difficulty, not to feel intimidated by his size. She pressed a hand to her queasy stomach. 'It was a mistake, OK? When I met you at the gallery I was just...I wasn't well, I didn't know what I was doing——'

'So you *have* decided to stop playing games. Wise choice.'

His grim approval made a little chill of fear feather through Olivia. Reality seemed to have slipped out of focus. Perhaps they actually *had* crashed and she was dead and this encounter was the beginning of the tortuous eternal wanderings of her wicked soul? God had chosen well if he had selected this man to be her personal devil, a constant reminder of earlier humiliations.

'I *am* going to be sick,' she said unsteadily.

'No, you're not.' This time it was an order, not a statement. Olivia gave a small cry as he bent and slid an arm behind her knees and swept her up against his chest. He held her easily, looking down at her pale face with a frown that made his tough face even more intimidating. 'You've lost a hell of a lot of weight in a few weeks. No wonder you look like a limp rag.'

Few weeks? Olivia was too confused to be annoyed by the insult to her appearance. It had been months since she had rid herself of his unwelcome interest. So long that she had almost completely forgotten him—except for those strange eyes and the golden hair. And his size. *Size*?

Apprehension stirred a vague memory. As he began to move towards the house she clutched at his chest. The sweater was so soft that it had to be cashmere and inadvertently her hand flattened, stroking over the expensive texture.

'Put me down,' she demanded weakly.

The thin mouth broke up, throwing curves into the rugged angles of his face, revealing a sensuous fullness of the lower lip that Olivia found as disconcerting as his grin. Last time, she realised, he hadn't smiled at all. Not even when...

'Put me down!' she said, trying to project the kind of commanding tone that Roz managed so effortlessly.

He didn't look at her, but his voice was full of gravelly humour at her attempt to assert herself. 'Who are you kidding, Kitten? You're so weak at the knees, you'd probably fall at my feet.'

He was so right that she began to struggle furiously. 'Stop calling me that!'

'Weak-kneed?'

'I hate you!' she said wildly, her thin face flushed with passion as she dug her fingers into his chest, wishing that she had the fingernails to penetrate the fine wool. It was like digging into stone.

'You don't know me well enough to claim that intimacy,' he said calmly.

'I know all I care to.' Her wildness left her as quickly as it had come, and she let her head slip so that it rested against his strong shoulder. 'What are you doing here, anyway?'

'Rescuing you from your own folly. It seems to be habit-forming.'

'I thought I was being sensible,' she said tiredly. 'How did I know that small planes would make me airsick? I've never flown in one before. And it wasn't my fault that the fuel-line or whatever it was got blocked——'

'You were lucky he was such a good pilot.'

Her own mouth curved humourlessly. 'Oh, yes, I have all the luck.'

Lulled by fatigue and the rocking of his long, rhythmic stride, Olivia closed her eyes as they mounted the steps to the huge solid cedar double doors that led into the house, only to open them again as she heard a clatter of heels and a crisp voice saying, 'What on earth are you doing, Jordan? I didn't know we were providing a carry-in service these days.'

Jordan? *Jordan*?

It wasn't such a common name that there could be any doubt, she realised in horror. Oh, *God* . . .

'Jordan? You're Jordan Pendragon!' she breathed, realising her mistake as he jolted to a halt just inside the door.

'I thought we'd decided that you were cured of your selective amnesia, Olivia,' he said grimly.

'Amnesia? Good God, Jordan, didn't I warn you she was unstable? This commission isn't supposed to be a social welfare benefit . . .'

Olivia blinked at the speaker. The acid tone of malicious amusement fixed the identity of the newcomer as Beverly Kelvin but she wasn't at all the sour-faced witch that had been brought to mind by Roz's contemptuous description. She was stunningly feminine, a tall, graceful brunette, her slender curves accentuated by the immaculate yet casual country elegance of her clothes. Her voice was throaty, soft and cultured and totally at odds with the sharpness of her words. She looked to be in her early twenties but she had to be older. That was no expression of dewy youth in her glossy brown eyes. The polished sophistication would act as a preservative, thought Olivia, congealing over the years to protect the smooth, seamlessly beautiful outer shell from the decay within. This woman would fiercely fight the onset of physical ageing and, judging from the hostile tension in the slender body, something precious had already been lost in the battle.

'Hello, Beverly.' Olivia was in such deep trouble that the other woman's malice made little impact. If he was Jordan Pendragon her charade was over before it had begun!

Her greeting was ignored. 'Isn't this carrying your penchant for waifs and strays rather to extremes, Jordan? If the girl can't even walk she can hardly be expected to work. And did I just see her vomiting in the flowers? She's not pregnant, by any chance, is she?'

'She's had a nasty shock, that's all. The plane that was bringing her here nearly crashed,' Jordan Pendragon said, in a deep, calm voice that displayed no irritation at the overt rudeness.

'What a pity.' The mocking glitter in Beverly's eyes made her expression of sympathy highly ambiguous. Olivia didn't doubt that a crash would have suited Beverly down to the ground—literally. 'Are you usually this accident-prone? Hardly a promising start, is it, Miss Marlow?'

Olivia wondered if she had already irretrievably blotted her copy-book by calling the woman by her first name. But then she thought of Roz's contempt and knew that frigid politeness was not a tactic her sister would have used. Brash and irritating friendliness would be more her style.

She felt Jordan's massive chest heave and cut in quickly, before he could answer in the affirmative—after all, hadn't he suggested as much himself? Acting purely on instinct, she nestled into Jordan's arms and purred, 'Oh, I don't know, *Bev,* some accidents can prove *very* promising...'

Instinct paid off. Beverly went rigid and something more than mere distaste flickered in her eyes. Tension crackled around them as Jordan said evenly, 'Could you ask Mike to bring Olivia's bags up to her room, please, Beverly? And arrange for a few sandwiches and some weak tea.'

'I really couldn't eat anything,' muttered Olivia, aware of the exchange of stares going on above her head. There was some emotion at work here that she didn't understand, not that she wanted to. Her own roller-coaster emotions were enough to cope with without involving herself in other people's.

'But you will.' Jordan was still looking at his cousin's fiancée as he spoke and the strange confrontation continued a few seconds longer until Beverly made a sharp sound of annoyance and turned on her heel, getting in one last thrust.

'Just make sure she isn't sick on the carpet. And give her a lesson in personal hygiene; she smells like one of your wretched goats!'

'You can put me down now,' said Olivia, without much hope of being obeyed, and was disconcerted when he did so.

'I told you last time, but obviously you didn't take any notice—it's not wise to antagonise Beverly just for the hell of it. She takes herself far too seriously to make a good enemy.'

'Surely that's a contradiction in terms,' said Olivia, pleased to find that her knees weren't as weak as she had been told.

'Some enemies can make fighting a pleasure,' said Jordan.

'I bet you never lost a fight in your life,' Olivia muttered dourly, obscurely unnerved by the silky quality of his words.

'Then you'd be wrong. Size isn't everything, Olivia. If it were you'd never have been able to kick me out of your apartment that night.'

She ducked her head to hide her reaction to the uncomfortable reminder and her nostrils twitched.

'She's right, I *do* smell terrible!' Olivia checked her clothing and groaned when she discovered the foul-smelling patch on the leg of her best black wool trousers. 'Oh, hell! I must have sat on something in the tray of that farmer's truck.'

'A little honest manure never hurt anyone.'

His amusement annoyed her. Olivia caught herself raising her middle finger to her mouth and hurriedly put it behind her back. Under the clear nail lacquer Roz had applied a coat of foul-tasting anti-biting lotion. Her mouth already tasted revolting; she didn't think her stomach could take any more punishment. Denied her nervous habit, Olivia grew even more restless under Jordan's steady stare. She wished she knew what he was thinking. Then she was glad she didn't. She had enough to cope with worrying about her *own* scurrying thoughts.

'Er—where am I going to be staying?' she enquired cautiously. Roz said she hadn't seen much of the house during her visit and Olivia wasn't sure how familiar she should be with her surroundings. 'I guess I should change before I meet Mr Pendragon... your father, that is.'

'I didn't think you were referring to me,' Jordan remarked drily. 'You never accorded me that much respect, even when we were strangers.'

'We still are strangers,' Olivia pointed out.

Again that terrifyingly sensual smile. 'You think so?' He continued blandly, 'We've put you on the third level this time, overlooking the lake. Very tranquil, very soothing to the nerves. There are quite a few stairs. Do you think you can make it or do you want me to carry you?'

Olivia squared her too-slim shoulders under her bulky sweater as she looked towards the stairway that curved from the warm terracotta-tiled entranceway high into a central gallery. A glass roof above the stairway sent light cascading in luminous waterfalls down the pale cream walls. 'I'm fine now,' she lied. Anything rather than let him touch her again.

By the time they got to the second level Olivia was labouring but again she refused an offer of assistance. When they finally reached the top level and Jordan guided her footsteps to the nearest room, she couldn't help a sigh of relief.

'You know what they say about pride, Olivia,' Jordan murmured as she moved past him into the bedroom, but she was too busy taking in the view to bother with a defensive reply.

She hadn't realised during the wretched drive that the Pendragon house was so near the Tongariro National Park. Perched high on a bushy outcrop above the ice-blue lake, the cantilevered rear took in a wide, sweeping vista. Olivia's bedroom had a high ceiling, its kauri rafters sloping down from windows at least four metres high. As she moved forward, drawn by those huge windows, she could look out across the wide, wind-ruffled lake. To her right, up the stony lake shore, she could see the distant smudge of the town of Taupo, to her left was the flat country around the mouth of the Tongariro River, and the rising bush-cloaked hills which guarded the triple snow-clad peaks of Mt Tongariro, Mt Ngauruhoe and Mt Ruapehu.

The double blue arc of lake and sky was reflected in the pale blue furnishings of the room, the vivid turquoise of the bedspread an accent to the paler shades in the thick wool carpet and the rag-rolled walls.

'When your bags come up you can change out of those trousers and we'll have them laundered for you. Normally you just put everything you want washed in the hamper in your bathroom. When you've had a rest I'll show you around the rest of the house so you can get your bearings; it's a little bit confusing with all the levels, even if you've visited before. And I'll show you the room which has been put aside for your paints and canvases. Any questions?'

Dozens. And not one of them could she ask, she realised in dismay. She could ring Roz but that would involve her in all sorts of awkward explanations, because she hadn't even told her twin about the mystery man who had rescued her from the art gallery. Jordan had not only physically stopped her from trying to drag her scorned works from the walls of the gallery, he had taken her back to her studio, given her a drink that had the impact of a bomb on her weakened body and then firmly put her to bed. When she had woken from a dead sleep a few hours later, she had been appalled to find him still there, stretched out beside her in a state of suspicious disarray. She had used all sorts of vile insults to get rid of him and then, still in the grip of deep depression, had started her painting frenzy. He had returned several times, but Olivia's wretchedness had denied his persistence. She had unplugged her phone and refused to answer the door. In the end her family had had to force her to seek medical help. Looking back, her behaviour had been appalling. She had literally slept with a man without even knowing his name!

Just some unfortunate gallery customer, she had thought. But he had known full well who *she* was. How had he felt when her name came up regarding the Pendragon commission? How much influence did he have with his father? Not much, obviously, or she wouldn't even be here. After the way she had carried on he couldn't have much of an opinion of her as a capable professional.

What had he said to Roz when she'd turned up for that first interview? More importantly, what had Roz, in her innocence, said to *him*? From his remarks about amnesia he must have taken that innocence to be a deliberate strategy and, fortunately, appeared to have been content to play along with it. Until now.

'When am I going to m—see your father?' She'd nearly said 'meet'. She would have to watch every word.

'When he wants to see you,' said Jordan drily. 'My father is a law unto himself. Painting his portrait is not going to be quite as easy as you anticipated.'

'I never thought it was going to be *easy*,' denied Olivia.

'I meant in terms of physically pinning my father down. He's not a man who enjoys being at the mercy of someone else's timetable, and he has little patience with what he terms the "artistic temperament".'

If that was an oblique reference to her recent past she chose to ignore it. 'That's why I'm here, isn't it, so that I can fit in with his schedule, rather than vice versa? As far as I'm concerned it's a natural arrangement. I'm not naïve. I have some experience painting the portraits of busy, important and impatient men.'

'I just thought I'd warn you. Father was on his best behaviour last time you were here, but he's not likely to keep that up for long. You might even find him somewhat ... hostile.'

Olivia's heart sank. Had he discussed her with his father, after all...? While she was mentally debating how to respond a slim, good-looking, dark-complexioned young man dropped her bags just inside the door, sketched a mocking salute to Jordan and directed a wink at Olivia as he withdrew.

'Why should he be hostile?' she demanded bravely. She might as well know what she was up against.

'Artists are not among his favourite people. Most of them he considers pretentious parasites or outright con-men.'

'Then why all the sponsorship, if he despises artists so much?' said Olivia suspiciously. Was Jordan, like Beverly, intent on sabotaging her small commission in order to put her out of the running for the larger one?

'Publicity. He has his eye on the New Year Honours list. He's wanted a knighthood for years and he figures that if they won't give him one for his services to the agricultural industry he'll buy one with his social philanthropy.'

So it was nothing to do with her personally. At least that still gave her a chance. For whatever reason, Jordan had held his peace.

'I can handle your father,' Olivia said, with more confidence than she felt.

His curiously coloured eyes drooped lazily. 'Then I'll be a fascinated observer, because nobody else has been able to manage it,' he murmured.

Olivia had had enough. 'Well, if you don't mind, I'll have that shower now.' She moved towards her bags and to her relief Jordan picked up the very unsubtle hint with a dutiful politeness that she didn't readily associate with him.

'I'll come and get you just before lunch and give you the grand tour on the way to the dining-room. If you need anything use the intercom. I think Tracey, our housekeeper, was away last time you were here. She's the one you'll get if you call the kitchen. She can deal with that stain for you. And do eat the snack she's going to send up; you look positively anorexic.' He frowned. 'You're not, are you?'

She bristled. In the darkest hour of her depressive illness she had never been suicidal. 'No, I'm not. It's just taking me a while to regain the weight I lost when I was ill.'

He flicked her a single all-encompassing stare before he left that suggested he wasn't entirely sure she was telling the truth. Stripping for her shower, Olivia had to admit that she looked a little like a scarecrow under her bulky clothes, so when she emerged from the luxurious en-suite bathroom to find a delicious array of snacks sitting on her bedside table she wolfed them down without a second thought for her uncertain stomach.

Still wearing the huge white bath-sheet that she had taken from the heated towel-rail, Olivia threw herself on the wide bed, revelling in the centrally heated warmth that denied the chilly reality of the snow-covered peaks that she could see from among her pillows. Olivia had seen her share of mountains—in Europe and in the States—but she still found the sight awesome, particularly the lazy evidence of the sleeping dragon, the belching steam drifting skywards from Mt Nguaruhoe, reminding the puny humans within its shadow of its claim to being New Zealand's most active volcano.

Sleeping dragon...Pendragon... Musing over the play on words, Olivia drifted from a light doze into the deeper reaches of sleep. When she jerked awake a couple of hours later, her brain groping to identify an alien sound, she felt a familiar flicker of panic that her sleep was still achingly dreamless, no vivid mind-pictures imprinting her consciousness, begging to be illuminated on canvas.

The alien sound was a gentle tapping on her door. Jordan? Olivia sat up muzzily, re-tucking the bath-towel that had drifted apart during her restless nap.

'Just a minute!' She needed some clothes to hide behind, but as she scurried towards her still unpacked suitcases the door opened.

Olivia's blush was wasted. The young woman who stood there was a total stranger. She, too, flushed.

'Oh, I'm sorry. I thought you said come in.'

'That's OK.' Bobbed blonde hair, gentle grey eyes, and a stolid frame that was probably the despair of her teenage vanity. Olivia racked her brains for an identity among the list Roz had given her and came up dismayingly blank.

'I'm Melissa Main, the housekeeper's daughter.' The introduction instantly allayed her panic. The girl smiled cautiously and Olivia realised that the sturdy practicality of her appearance masked a shy diffidence. 'Mum just sent me to check that you knew about the mealtimes. We usually serve lunch at one and dinner at eight. Breakfast is anytime you like it, here or in the dining-room...'

Olivia looked at her watch and grimaced. 'I didn't mean to sleep so long. Jordan was going to show me around before lunch but I suppose it's too late now.'

'He told Mum he looked in on you earlier and decided that you needed the rest more than the tour.' Melissa's smile was more relaxed. Jordan had looked in? Olivia recalled how her towel had come apart and groaned inwardly. 'I thought I'd better come and warn you. Mr Pendragon senior has a real thing about punctuality. Do you want me to help you unpack?'

'Thanks.' Olivia accepted gratefully. Used to travelling light, she had brought more than she had planned, for Roz had gone through her bags and insisted on adding several more scintillating outfits of her own. Chatting lightly to put the girl at her ease, she learned that Melissa, now nearly seventeen, had been three when her mother had taken on the job of housekeeper to the Pendragons, and had grown up on the estate, a fact that explained her unconsciously proprietorial attitude towards the family. Olivia had no hesitation in asking her advice about the immediate problem of what to wear, thereby making a friend for life.

'The family don't dress for lunch but Mr Pendragon doesn't really approve of women in trousers and Miss Kelvin is always impeccable.' The hint of acidity gave Olivia the reason for the girl's initial diffidence. Obviously Beverly hadn't endeared herself to the housekeeper's daughter and Olivia could guess why. A snob, Roz had said. And snobs didn't hobnob with staff. Encouraged by Olivia's grin of understanding, Melissa murmured, 'This green dress would be prefect...'

She held it up. It was one of Roz's, of course. Olivia slipped into the blue-tiled bathroom to put it on and eyed herself critically in the full-length mirror. The muted sea-green suited her and, where the jersey knit would have strained at the seams six months ago, now it merely skimmed her curves. In fact, it even looked a little loose in places. Olivia averted her critical gaze. She intended to be nothing but positive from now on, cultivating a healthy aggression. She applied her usual light make-up and had to wash it off and start again when she discovered that the newly revealed hollows of her face required softer contouring than the old, smoothly rounded version. She settled for just brushing her hair and drawing the thick red waves back from her face with a couple of black combs. The result didn't have quite the panache that Roz would have achieved with the same props but no one was going to notice.

When she emerged from the bathroom she found Melissa had finished hanging up her clothes, and was moving towards the door.

'Would you mind waiting a few moments, just until I get my shoes on?' Olivia asked. 'Then you can show me the way to the dining-room; I'm sure to get lost otherwise, I have a hopeless sense of direction...' Olivia's feet were about the only things that hadn't shrunk with her illness. They were still half a size larger than Roz's and she winced as she eased her feet into the overly snug green shoes. Apart from a comfortable collection of well-worn boots and sneakers, she possessed only one pair of good high heels—plain black court shoes that Roz had regarded with scorn.

Melissa was apologetic. 'I wasn't trying to rush you. Jordan told us all about your crash. I'm sure they'll understand if you're a few minutes late...'

'That's OK, I'm ready now.' But not ready enough, she acknowledged. Since she didn't have access to her sister's fund of acquired knowledge, she needed to start building up her own. 'Is everyone here for lunch, do you know?'

'Except for William. He's in Wellington for the week. He won't be back until Saturday.' Olivia gave an internal sigh of relief at the temporary reprieve from pretending to know yet another stranger. Her encouraging smile seemed to work because Melissa carried on, 'Actually he's hardly been here at all over the last three weeks. He has tremendous responsibilities now, you know.'

Olivia heard the sighing hint of hero worship, confirmed by Melissa's artless familiarity. William, whatever else he was, was evidently no snob. 'He's supposed to be head of the company now, except Mr Pendragon still tries to run it himself even though he officially retired last year. He still expects his orders to be carried out even if *he* hasn't consulted William. It's not that Mr Pendragon doesn't trust him, it's just that he won't let *go*, if you know what I mean. It's very frustrating for both of them...'

'I imagine it must be,' Olivia murmured, amused by that mature perception in one so young, her attention partly distracted by the beautiful cream walls that were crying out for some sort of ornamentation. They were a stark testimony to Jordan's sardonic words. Roz had said the house was built ten years ago, yet no one who was a true art-lover could have so long resisted all this enticingly blank wall-space. As they reached the second floor several pieces that she had been too weary to notice on the way up did appear on the high walls of the gallery—mostly, she noticed glumly, by John Ferris. 'What about Jordan?'

'What do you mean?'

Olivia's attention snapped back, cautioned by Melissa's innocent puzzlement. 'Does he support William?' she asked vaguely.

'Oh, they get on OK but Jordan pretty much stays away these days. Even if he did want to help William I don't think he could. Mr Pendragon is probably *more* likely to veto an idea if he thinks that Jordan favours it. He's never forgiven Jordan for leaving the company... It absolutely infuriates him that even though Jordan doesn't show any interest in the company any more he still won't give up his seat on the board.' Melissa seemed to enjoy the idea of the old man being infuriated. On the subject of his irascibility Roz had obviously not exaggerated.

'Why doesn't he just vote Jordan out? Surely he has enough clout.' So, even if Jordan *had* expressed any negative opinions about Olivia, she would still be here, if only as a pawn in a power-play between father and son.

A gleam of mischief lit Melissa's soft eyes. 'He can't. All the children have voting shares but when Jordan was born, a son and heir after four lowly daughters, Alun rushed out and placed another big parcel of voting shares in trust for him. And Jordan's mother, Flora, left him *her* shares, too. Everything was OK while Mr Pendragon controlled the income from the trust, but when Jordan came of age things got awkward.'

Melissa was relishing her role as story-teller, safe in the knowledge that what she was telling Olivia was common knowledge to the rest of the interested world. 'He has just enough shares to retain his seat if he has the support of all his sisters, which he so far always has. He normally gives William the proxy when they need a full vote so it's never really been a problem, except for Mr Pendragon, who likes to be in control. He could have cut Jordan out by letting the corporation go public but of course that would mean letting shares go outside the family...'

'How does William feel about it?'

'Well, I suppose he feels a bit guilty that he took what was supposed to be Jordan's place, so he tries not to let Alun corner him into taking sides.' Melissa scowled. 'But ever since he got engaged to Miss Kelvin, well...she makes it really difficult sometimes...'

Olivia felt rather than saw Melissa's tentative sideways glance, as if judging her reaction. Was she afraid she had said too much? And yet she didn't stop there, and suddenly Olivia knew that her blunt informativeness had been Melissa's way to leading up to this significant moment.

'Miss Kelvin is...well, she isn't directly involved in the business or anything but she's known the family for years and is very—well—*possessive* if you know what I mean, and not only about William... She can get quite nasty if she thinks people are trying to, well, edge her out...' Melissa took a deep breath, scarlet by now but doggedly determined to stop beating about the bush as she half whispered, 'She has...she has this idea that...that you've got your hooks into Jordan and——'

'She thinks I've *what*?' gasped Olivia incredulously.

'I—I'm sorry, I'm not prying or anything,' Melissa stammered. 'It's just that when she found out about your affair with Jordan——'

'My *what*?'

Melissa's courage failed her. She hugged herself miserably. 'Oh, dear, I shouldn't have said anything. Mum will *kill* me! Please forget I even mentioned it—I didn't mean to upset you, I only wanted to help...I know that you and Jordan haven't told anyone—but that's why I—I just thought you ought to know that *she* knows! The dining-room is through there.' She pointed towards the full-length double doors at the end of the hallway, and scuttled away, leaving Olivia trailing dumbly into the gaping jaws of the unknown.

She had thought she had been deserted by her dreams, but now it was reality that was conspicuously absent. She and Jordan Pendragon having an affair! Whose nightmarish imagination had conjured up *that* ridiculous fantasy?

CHAPTER THREE

OLIVIA toyed nervously with her soup spoon. The thick, creamy seafood bisque smelled delicious but her earlier enthusiasm for food had deserted her. The tense atmosphere at the lunch table certainly provided no incentive for digestion, but eating would definitely be a safer bet than conversing. Conversation was a potential minefield. Even the most innocent remarks were primed by her guilt to explode with hidden meanings. Not that the Pendragons were very long on innocence. The antagonisms ebbing and flowing around the table indicated a host of hidden resentments.

Olivia's first sight of Alun Pendragon had been an inordinate relief. Roz was right. He was a portrait waiting to be painted . . . a smooth, ageless face, a thick head of grey hair, a neatly trimmed moustache. He would have been extremely handsome in his youth and his arrogance proclaimed that he still knew himself to be an attractive man, despite his advanced age. He wasn't a big man and his elegant suit emphasised his sleek and dapper appearance, but the rest of him was certainly larger than life, enabling him to dominate the room despite his size. His voice and his gestures were aggressively expansive and his sharp sapphire-blue eyes snapped with restless energy.

Fascination warred with aversion in Olivia's mind. The first words out of Alun Pendragon's mouth had made her hackles rise. She rarely made impulsive judgements about people but she had the sinking feeling that she and her subject were destined to dislike each other.

'Humph! So you did arrive after all,' he had barked, sounding almost disappointed as Olivia had drifted numbly into the huge dining-room that jutted out over the lake.

Her dazed feeling of fatalistic calm was shattered by his rudeness and she had instinctively responded in kind.

'It's delightful to see you again, too, Mr Pendragon,' she murmured with sweet insincerity.

'What?' Alun Pendragon stared at her suspiciously before abruptly turning his elegant back to demand of Beverly. 'I thought you said she wasn't coming?'

Beverly raised a delicately curved eyebrow. True to Melissa's prediction, she was dressed as if she had just stepped out of the pages of *Country Life*.

'She almost didn't. Her plane nearly crashed on the way down here.'

She made it sound as if it were entirely Olivia's own fault and the elder Pendragon frowned accusingly as he swung back.

'You're a *pilot*?'

Definitely a male chauvinist pig of the highest order of swine, decided Olivia, correctly interpreting the disapproving glitter in the shrewd blue eyes. She wished she could smugly assure him that she regularly flew 747s, but she was already burdened with enough lies to remember. However, she sensed that if she showed that his aggression upset her he would take it as a sign of weakness and exploit it ruthlessly.

'No. I appreciate the convenience, not to mention the poetry of flight, but the mechanics don't interest me at all,' she said calmly.

Alun Pendragon's expression shifted and he stiffened. Olivia wondered what fresh prejudice she had blundered into. Weren't women supposed to be capable of answering back? Or was he—her courage quailed—preparing to fling her supposed raging affair with his son in her face?

'What are *you* doing here?' he rasped.

Olivia blinked, her dizzy sense of disorientation returning. Hadn't they just *had* this conversation?

'I was under the impression that this was the family home. I didn't realise I needed a personal invitation.'

The deep, velvety sarcasm shivered down her spine, tingles of awareness spreading over the width of her back. Olivia refused to give in to the compulsion to look over her shoulder, giving herself a few extra moments to compose her expression before she had to face her *supposed* lover.

'Since when do you ever honour invitations from your family?' his father growled.

'When they're couched as such. It's being *ordered* to appear I take exception to.' Olivia could see Jordan now, from the corner of her wary eye. He wasn't wearing a suit or a tie but his dark brown trousers and white shirt topped with a tweed jacket could be considered a concession to his father's sartorial standards, although somehow he still managed to look...undisciplined. Yes, that was the word. Like a painting roughed out on the canvas, the bold outlines refusing to conform to any preconceptions, the finer detail lost in the brutal impact of the whole.

'Now, Alun, as it happened *I* was the one who suggested that he come,' Beverly smoothly stepped between the two men. 'It's not healthy for him to be in that place of his while all that work is going on. The dirt and dust flying about is appalling——'

'It was his own choice to move out there.' Alun's glare didn't waver from his son. 'If his health is at risk he knows exactly who to blame.' He abandoned the contemptuous third person to address his son directly. 'I told you at the time that that place wasn't fit for human habitation, but you wouldn't listen then, boy, and now you're paying the price for ignoring good advice. You had a perfectly good suite of rooms here, all the luxury and privacy you could want, but that wasn't enough for you. No, you had to go and live in that rotting old cowshed—a choice fairly indicative of your entire lifestyle—and now you want to pour good money after bad just for the sake of preserving your pride. That place was built to house cattle and that's all it'll ever be fit for. Why don't you just admit you made a mistake and come back where you belong...?'

His smug triumph was so ill-concealed that Olivia wondered whether he was deliberately goading his son, under the guise of offering to heal a breach in family relations. She braced herself for an explosive reply. Jordan didn't look like the kind of man to meekly turn the other cheek to verbal slaps at his pride.

'Since you've never admitted making a mistake in your life, you're hardly in a position to offer advice on the subject.' The mildness of Jordan's tone was deceptive, his father's bridling colour attesting to the accuracy of the thrust.

Beverly's confidence seemed to thrive on the bristling hostility. She calmly ordered the seating and signalled for the meal to be served with a gesture reminiscent of royalty. To her dismay Olivia was trapped between Alun Pendragon and Beverly, directly opposite the unnerving Jordan. She had decided that it would be wisest to keep a low profile during the meal but it seemed that being a guest didn't exempt her from having to take sides in an alien war.

'I don't suppose *you* live in a barn, do you, Miss Marlow?' Alun Pendragon demanded with what he probably thought was a pleasant smile, as she settled into the padded seat of the carved kauri chair and smiled her thanks at the plump, motherly looking woman placing a steaming terrine of soup next to a basket of floury, fresh-baked rolls on the table. Tracey's resemblance to her daughter was unmistakable.

'Uh—no, I have a very nice studio apartment in the city...' she said, uneasily conscious that she was being used as bait.

'By yourself?'

'Mostly. Sometimes friends come to live in for a while——' Beverly's delicate revulsion suddenly invested Olivia's innocent words with wildly promiscuous connotations and she added firmly, 'Mostly other artists who want to work in my studio. And members of my family visit off and on, when they're in town...'

Alun Pendragon's eyes sparked briefly at the mention of her famous family but he was intent on pursuing his own point. 'Yes, yes, but your surroundings aren't *vital* to you. A *true* artist should be able to work in any surroundings, wouldn't you say?'

'Well...' She wasn't sure where this was leading, and she didn't like the avid expectancy in the old man's face. She made the mistake of flicking a glance across the table to find Jordan leaning back in his chair, watching her, arms crossed casually over his mighty chest, an expression of cynical amusement lighting the odd-coloured eyes. Whatever obscure game his father was playing he knew what it was, but wasn't going to step in and help her learn the rules.

Olivia's eyes widened at a sudden thought. Hadn't Roz told her that Jordan preferred men to women? The impact of meeting him again had been so stunning that she had forgotten that titbit of information! Vague, unwelcome memories drifted across her appalled consciousness. Hadn't she practically tried to rape him on that awful night they met? The single drink he had given her to calm her down had had the opposite effect. It had acted like a powerful drug on her weakened system, blurring her mind and burning out her protective inhibitions. Desperate to at least be successful as a woman where she had failed utterly as an artist, Olivia had boldly tried to seduce him. Instead he had put her to bed as if she were a naughty child, not even turning a hair when she had insisted on sleeping in the nude. He had fended off her unwelcome advances and tucked her firmly under the bedclothes before settling on top of them beside her, trapping her further. *That* was why her humiliated fury the next morning had been so intense. In hindsight she knew she had probably been far from alluring in her wretched state but his rejection had none the less crucified her already tormented ego.

The thought that it might not have been Olivia the woman he was rejecting but women in general didn't appease her at all. In fact, it fuelled her anger. Was this ridiculous suggestion of an affair between them a deliberate smoke-screen to hide his sexual preferences from his family? How dared he use her like that? Her eyes went as dark as a stormy sea as she glared across the table at him and said pointedly,

'Since art is an expression of one's inner self I suppose that environment *is* only incidental, but everyone has their own habits and . . . *preferences* . . .'

Jordan seemed unmoved by her thrust, so she probed further. 'I think the only real necessity for an artist is to be true to oneself, however difficult that might be, or however much it might put you in conflict with others.'

This time she did get a reaction, but not the discomfort she had expected. Jordan's humour lost its cynicism and the strange tawny gold sheen that tinted one eye suddenly seemed to spread to both, warming the cool blue to a sensual hazel. His smile seemed to be sending her an intimate message that she couldn't interpret. Olivia dropped her gaze to his hands, which were resting at ease on the pristine white tablecloth on either side of his soup bowl.

Unlike his father's manicured neatness, Jordan's hands were as big and bold as the rest of him, rough-cut and muscular, covered with crisp gold hair and decorated with numerous minute gashes and calluses. They were hands which made no apology for the physical labour they performed. Olivia remembered hazily what it felt like to have those big hands moving over her body, dealing with buttons and zips, restraining her own wandering hands, cupping her chin to push her gently but inexorably away when she had tried to kiss him. Olivia hurriedly looked up again and found him still watching her. To her shock she felt a violent blush suffuse her skin—she, who con-

sidered herself a fully qualified, world-weary
sophisticate!

The tawny blue eyes narrowed instantly under shifting
gold brows and suddenly she was aware of the penetrating intelligence lurking beneath the brawn. Taunting
him was a rotten idea. She had bared more than her
body to him that dreadful night. She couldn't remember
exactly how much of her soul she had bawled out on his
broad shoulder, how many of her sins she had confessed, but she knew it was enough to give him a wicked
advantage. Quickly she returned her attention to Alun
Pendragon. To her dismay he, too, was monitoring his
son's reaction.

Beverly, in contrast, was staring at Olivia, no doubt
vaulting to her own conclusions for her blushes.

'So you're an idealist,' she said acidly. 'How quaint.
From your CV I would have thought you'd have long
lost your innocence. You were with an artist's commune
in Auckland before you went overseas, weren't you?
With that Logan Firth person—the one there was all that
scandal about recently...something about under-age girls
he was "tutoring" in more than just art? And then two
years living with the great Diego Martinez...that must
have been a very *broadening* experience for you...'

Olivia had long given up protesting people's er-
roneous assumption that she had been Diego's mistress.
If it hadn't been for Melissa's untimely warning of the
other woman's malice Olivia's bewilderment would have
made her vulnerable, but even so the reference to Logan
made her wince. She *had* been as green as grass at twenty,
when she had joined Logan's artistic commune,
otherwise she would have seen through the charismatic
charm that masked his own lack of talent and emotional
depth. She had been in love with life and art and had
thrown herself eagerly into the heady experience of being
flattered and desired by a glamorously sophisticated older
man. But although she had lost her virginity to Logan's
determined seduction she had not really lost her heart.

That had been merely bruised by disillusionment when she had been offered an arts council grant to study in Paris and Logan had suggested she cheat the system by splitting the grant with him. The fact that he believed she should be happy to sacrifice some of her precious art classes so that he could hitch a free ride on her talent had opened her eyes to the fact that his interest in her was considerably less than his self-interest. She wasn't surprised to hear about the scandal. At their final, angry parting Logan had taunted her with the fact that, at twenty-one, she was 'getting a bit long in the tooth' for him, anyway.

'Yes, it was,' she agreed quietly. 'I admire Diego tremendously.'

'As an artist or as a man?' Beverly prodded with a coyness that was at odds with the steely glint in her eye.

'Both.' Olivia denied the innuendo victory over her simmering temper.

'After living such an *exciting* life, it must have been difficult for you to leave the object of such devoted admiration and come back to New Zealand. I suppose that's why you've produced so little work this past year. What made you decide to break up such a *rewarding* relationship? Did "artistic differences" lead to you and Mr Martinez going your separate ways?' The innocent use of the stock gossip-column phrase normally used to cloak a myriad libellous suggestions gave Beverly's words a barbed purpose. The woman herself was about as innocent as the serpent in the garden of Eden, Olivia thought grimly, deciding to haul up the big guns.

'Oh, no, something much more mundane, I'm afraid. My brother, Richard, was getting married. Our family is close, despite the conflicting demands of our respective careers. If I hadn't come back I think my mother would have come across to fetch me. And then I was ill for a while and my parents insisted on my moving back home. My mother even stalled her career so that she could baby me . . . but she's had a marvellous offer of a film part in Sydney so it's just as well I've flown the nest again...'

Olivia smiled confidingly at Alun Pendragon as she dangled the bait under his nose and this time he snapped. Usually modest about her famous family, Olivia felt that in the circumstances her parents would forgive her a little harmless gossiping, especially on the subject of the knighthood her father had received in the latest Queen's Birthday Honours list. It was a subject that held the elder Pendragon riveted.

By the time Olivia's three-quarters-full soup bowl was replaced by a crisp mixed salad and strips of chilled rare roast beef the knots in her stomach had relaxed enough to enable her to nibble tentatively at the offering, until Beverly suddenly decided that if she couldn't beat her host's interest down she would share it.

'I remember seeing your sister on stage a couple of years ago when I was in London—doing some very dark and gothic Jacobean play where almost everyone died horribly. You only have the one sister, don't you?'

'Yes, but I have a couple of great sisters-in-law,' said Olivia evasively, her heart beginning to pound hectically in her chest. The last person she wanted to talk about was Roz. Did any of them even know they were twins? The toes that she had eased gratefully out of the ill-fitting shoes at the start of the meal curled into the thick pale grey carpet under the dining-table. Hastily she began to search for the discarded shoes. Grace in victory, dignity in defeat...it was something of a family motto. Olivia was a little short on all counts at the moment. She might need the added height of Roz's heels to give her some borrowed confidence. Stepping into her sister's shoes...the phrase was literally as well as figuratively true, she thought guiltily. She skated her stockinged sole across the cut pile and inadvertently up the leg of the table.

Across from her Jordan straightened abruptly from his lazy slouch, a look of incredulous surprise crossing his face.

Table legs don't wear trousers! Aghast, Olivia realised what she had done and snatched back her foot, tucking her leg as far back under the chair as she could manage. Jordan's shock was swiftly superseded by a hard stare of speculation that made her cringe and she widened her eyes, silently pleading with him not to say anything. His expression didn't soften. Did he think she had done it on *purpose*, for goodness' sake? If only she could sink blissfully through the floor... but she could just imagine what Jordan would think if she began to disappear below the table! He would probably imagine she was bent on performing some new, wild indecency on his highly suspecting person. She went hot at the thought.

'Is the horse-radish sauce too much for you, Olivia?' Beverly asked, thankfully misinterpreting their guest's flush. 'Tracey makes it very concentrated because she knows we like it that way.'

We? Beverly obviously already considered herself a Pendragon. Olivia couldn't understand how she could possibly pose a threat to that monumental confidence. Even if by some wild stretch of the imagination she *were* Jordan's lover, how could that threaten Beverly's position of influence as queen of the household? It would evidently take a full-scale palace revolution to accomplish that!

'Oh, I imagine Olivia enjoys a dash of dangerous spice in her life,' Jordan murmured blandly, his eyes containing a hint of puzzlement as they lingered on her hot face.

'What makes you say that?' Beverly darted suspiciously, aware of some silent communication that eluded her.

Jordan shrugged, massive shoulders moving fluidly under the wool tweed. He needed no padding to emphasise the masculine cut of his jacket. 'Instinct.'

Alun Pendragon made a sound halfway between a snort and a growl and bullied his way back to centre stage. 'Your instincts haven't proved very sound in the past, boy, especially about women. He and Beverly were engaged once,' he informed Olivia, with a mind-blowing frankness that made Melissa appear the epitome of discretion. 'But he misjudged her loyalty to this family the way he misjudged everything else. He thought that she would approve his selfish irresponsibility, put up with his outrageous demands. He wanted to "go back to the land". Back! He'd never been there in the first place!' The rasping outrage seemed as fresh as if the betrayal had only just occurred. 'I worked to build this family into something and he throws it all away on some cock-eyed notion of "finding himself". That sort of nonsense is for no-hopers going nowhere. I've always known exactly who you are. My son. And no son of mine is going to deny his heritage. One day you'll have to admit that your rightful place is here with us.'

Jordan didn't appear to be concerned about having his inadequacies paraded before a virtual stranger. 'And one day *you're* going to have to face up to the fact that I'm not interested in your dynasty-building.'

Jordan and Beverly had been engaged? Olivia was still struggling with her shock. No wonder there were so many cross-currents between them. *Beverly and Jordan*? Was he the reason for the bitterness that seemed to marble her character? Had she really walked out when he chose not to follow in his father's footsteps, or had there been another reason? His probable homosexuality? But if Beverly knew about *that* then she would have known that he and Olivia couldn't possibly be lovers. And now Beverly was to marry her former fiancé's cousin, the heir to his misfortune... Surely any resentment should all be on Jordan's side? Just contemplating the tortuous possibilities made Olivia's head ache. She had enough problems herself. She didn't need to worry about the Pendragons as well!

'You were the one who limited my choices and forced a show-down, not I,' Jordan was saying evenly. 'All or nothing, you said. I could follow my own dreams or subjugate them once and for all to your obsession with establishing a Pendragon empire. You forgot, deliberately, I don't doubt, that part of my heritage dwells in the Welsh mining valleys, maybe the best part. You fought like hell to drag yourself out of one prison of expectation, only to try and lock me into another——'

'I haven't forgotten! It's *because* I haven't forgotten that I expect better things of you. I don't want my children, or my children's children, to know the kind of deprivation I had to suffer. You talk about the claustrophobia of wearing a suit—boy, you don't know what the word means. If I learned anything in those bloody mines it was that power is an impartial tool. It works for anyone strong enough to seek it and wield it. Only a coward, or a fool, runs away from the chance...!'

'I'd rather be acknowledged as a coward or a fool, if that's what I am, than a pawn in someone else's power game,' Jordan replied evenly and for the first time Olivia glimpsed a resemblance between the two men in their stony expressions. Stubborn, tenacious, strong-willed, they would be ruthlessly loyal friends and implacable enemies. She shivered.

Fruit and cheese was served during the obdurate silence and Olivia thought that perhaps it was her turn to try to neutralise hostilities.

'Do you have a particular time of day that you want to set aside for me to begin the portrait, Mr Pendragon, or did you have in mind just working straight through until it's finished?' she enquired pleasantly.

The sapphire-blue eyes looked blankly at her for a moment, as if he had forgotten who she was, then the grey eyebrows lowered irritably. 'I don't have the time to waste sitting around doing nothing, Miss Marlow. I'm not on the scrap-heap yet, you know. You'll just have to wait until I'm free. I'll let you know when.'

Don't call me, I'll call you? Olivia hid her chagrin at this proof that Jordan was right about the difficulties she would face. 'You won't have to sit absolutely still, Mr Pendragon, I just want to get some quick mood sketches first——'

'I don't want this thing rushed——'

'These are only preliminary sketches, to give me an idea of the best pose and background——'

'I know what pose I want and I don't want any background. Just me.'

It figured. 'Why don't I try out a few ideas?'

'That's what I'm paying you for. You just go ahead and do that without me.' He waved a relieved hand at her. 'My time is a great deal more valuable than yours, young lady; I can't be hanging round a studio waiting for inspiration to oblige you——'

If there was anything worse than a temperamental sitter it was a reluctant one. Olivia was aware of Beverly's superior smirk. A militant glitter entered her soft mist-green eyes. She was fed up with being pushed around by fate and a guilty conscience...and the arrogant Pendragons.

'That won't be necessary. It's not the way I like to work,' she lied smoothly. After all, *her* way hadn't worked for months. Maybe it was time for a change. 'In fact you don't need to set any special time aside for me at all. I'll just observe you going through your normal daily routine——'

'You want to follow me around all day with a sketch-pad!' Alun Pendragon almost blanched at the notion. 'I can't have you invading my privacy. A lot of the information that I deal with is highly confidential——'

'I'm very discreet——'

'I don't like distractions when I'm trying to concentrate.'

'Good. Neither do I,' said Olivia firmly. 'That's settled, then. After all, Mr Pendragon, the sooner I begin the sooner I'll be finished. Shall we say I join you first thing tomorrow morning?'

'First thing in the morning I have an appointment with my lawyer,' Alun Pendragon growled, torn between the logic of her words and his obvious loathing to give ground.'

'I'll be as quiet and unobtrusive as a mouse,' promised Olivia.

A muffled sound that could have been a snort drifted across the table, but Olivia refused to look at Jordan, sure she would find him smiling the cynically mocking smile that made her blood-pressure escalate. She had been anything but unobtrusive around him. Every time they met it seemed she was making a thorough fool of herself.

'I don't like nagging women.' A sullen trace of the Welsh finally edged the cultured vowels.

'And I don't like indecisive men,' said Olivia sweetly.

'Indecisive?' He almost spluttered in his outrage and she took advantage of his momentary shock.

'I thought you wanted a portrait painted, but obviously you're not quite sure. If you've changed your mind...'

The merest suggestion of vacillation triggered his automatic denial-response. 'Of course I haven't changed my mind! I'll see you tomorrow morning at nine sharp...and be prepared for a long day! I may be seventy but I've got a whole lot more drive and ambition than a lot of men half my age...' Here he couldn't resist a jabbing look at his son. 'Indecisive? You're going to see just how wrong that assumption is, young lady.' He pushed away from the table and stood up. 'Now you may all have time to sit about talking nonsense, but I have work to do. Jordan, come along, I want to see you in my study——'

Olivia relaxed, careful not to let her triumph at the success of her tilt at his vanity show. She was buoyed by a sudden optimism. If Jordan didn't live on the premises, she had realised, then she would only be obliged to endure his company at the occasional meal. It should be fairly easy to avoid being alone with him . . .

'Sorry, Father, I promised I'd show Olivia her studio. I'll come and see you before I leave.'

'Nonsense, Jordan.' Beverly also rose. 'There's no need to bother with that chore, when you have more important things to do. I can show Olivia where she'll be working.'

Olivia lowered her eyes demurely, hiding her delight. So she was relegated to a *chore*. That suited her fine. Beverly was better than a guard dog.

'Perhaps. But I think Olivia could prefer to stick to our *original* arrangement. Wouldn't you, Olivia?' The words were softly spoken but Olivia's eyes jerked up, her mental grin crumbling at the cool, challenging confidence of his expression. Blackmail. On the surface his words sounded like a perfectly innocent enquiry but the potential underlying threat was unmistakable. If she didn't agree with his suggestion, there was no telling what he might choose to let slip about her. She held out under that steady regard for a few brave seconds, then muttered her unwilling consent.

She hardly even heard the short, sharp altercation that followed. That Jordan would get his way seemed a foregone conclusion. And that by giving in to him this time she was paving the way for future forced compliance to his will was equally clear. She beat down her panic. She would just have to brazen it out and try not to let him see how very vulnerable she was.

As Alun Pendragon strode stiff-backed away and Beverly lacerated the air with daggers of suspicion Olivia began to rise, and then subsided again in her chair, remembering her wayward shoes. As she summoned the courage to bend down and see where the wretched things were she felt leather nudge against her toes. She squeezed her feet back into their mini torture-chambers, refusing to thank the man across the table for his discreet assistance. Discretion was a blackmailer's trade mark. At least he had demonstrated that he knew she hadn't been running her feet up his trouser legs for the sheer fun of it!

And at least, she told herself bracingly, there was one thing she could be absolutely certain of: he couldn't be planning to blackmail her in the hope of obtaining sexual favours!

Half an hour later all Olivia's concrete certainties were in ruins.

She stared at Jordan in outrage, her admiration and pleasure in the compact yet well-equipped studio adjoining the back of the house swallowed up in a flood of furious indignation.

'What do you mean you're not gay? Of course you're gay!' she yelled at him, her electric fury arcing and sizzling across the narrow space between them.

'Am I? Then I obviously have no desire to do *this* . . .'

For the second time in a few hours Olivia found herself in Jordan Pendragon's arms, but this time he was not being gentle. Before his mouth closed fiercely over hers, Olivia had a fleeting glimpse of the ice-cold male wrath freezing the odd-coloured eyes.

His eyes might be icy, she discovered, but his mouth was hot. Hot and very, very expert . . .

The dragon was breathing a fire that was melting every bone in his captive's body!

CHAPTER FOUR

IT WAS his fault, of course. Up until that moment Olivia's self-control, though wobbly, had survived Jordan's unpredictability. At first he had acted the role of the perfect host as he had led the way to her temporary working quarters through what seemed like a maze of terracotta-tiled corridors with high, arching white walls punctuated by dozens of oddly shaped little windows.

'Whoever designed this house must have a very interesting mind,' Olivia had commented, liking the crazy complexity of it all.

'Thank you.' Jordan had taken off his jacket and hooked it over one shoulder. He had no tie to remove and his collar was already open but, striding easily beside her, he released a second button on his shirt as if even the smallest restriction of his physical freedom annoyed him. Glancing at his rugged profile, Olivia saw the taut corner of his mouth had curved upwards with the merest hint of smugness.

'*You* designed this house?' Disbelief dripped from every syllable.

'Along with the builder, a friend of mine. In fact he's doing the renovations on my barn. The original house on this site burned down about fourteen years ago.'

Fourteen years ago the design for this house would have been almost revolutionary! 'And your *father* asked you to design a new one for him? Why on earth would he do that?' Her bewilderment, verging on accusation, could have been interpreted as an insult, if Jordan hadn't already witnessed her warm approval of her environment.

'He didn't ask. I offered.'

'And he *let* you, even though you weren't an architect?' Olivia was still incredulous. Alun Pendragon

58

didn't come across as an indulgent man, especially where his son was concerned. 'Wasn't that taking a big risk?'

'Not really. Although I was responsible for the concept we had an architect and engineer draw up the final building plans. Besides, my father likes to go out on a limb every now and then. He may consider himself an arch-conservative but there's a capricious streak in his nature that likes to throw a curve when it's least expected.'

'If you can design houses like this what are you doing——?' She stopped, annoyed with herself for revealing her curiosity.

'Wallowing with the beasts in the field?'

'I wasn't going to say that. It just seems to me that a lot of enjoyment went into the creation of this house...'

'I did enjoy it... at the time. Now I enjoy farming. I like variety in my life. Don't you?'

'I suppose so,' said Olivia dubiously, not quite sure what the pointed remark was supposed to convey. 'But it's a shame when a potential talent is ignored...'

'You think I have potential?'

He had stopped before a plain panelled-wood door at the end of a blind corridor. Olivia was sure that he was amused but she didn't know why, and the resentment she had pushed to a back burner began to simmer again.

'Yes. The potential to be even more arrogant than your father.' Her wild shot clipped the mocking smile neatly off his face. His thick blond brows lowered as he turned and abruptly threw the door open. Lost for words? Olivia didn't think so. He chose his silences as cleverly as he chose his words. Now she felt guilty for her insult to her host and patron... even though she had been goaded into it!

Her eyes flicked past him and Olivia momentarily forgot her annoying companion. With an exclamation of pleasure she brushed past him into the long room. The studio was part of the house, yet separate, a narrow finger pointing away at an odd tangent. The long windowed wall faced not the distracting beauty of Lake Taupo, but the lushly rugged greenery of a rising slope and overhead three large, flat skylights allowed natural daylight to flood the room evenly. At each end of the room timber shelving above solid wood waist-level benches were stocked with various art-supplies. Olivia saw that her own paints and canvases were neatly stored among the rest.

'It's perfect!' she said, resisting the tug of those tidily stacked shelves. Too tidy. She longed to run her hands along them, rearrange everything into the precisely ordered confusion that she worked best among. 'What is this place normally used for?'

'As you see.' Jordan spread his big hands.

Olivia was startled. 'A *studio*? But I thought your father had no time for artists?'

'My mother enjoyed dabbling. There was a small studio in the original house.'

'But your mother's been dead for forty years!' Olivia blurted out.

'Didn't you pay attention during your biology lessons, Olivia? Too busy doodling sketches in the margins?' He startled her again with his change of subject.

It was precisely what had happened. Olivia glared at him. She didn't see what her miserable school marks in everything but art had to do with the here and now.

'I'm only thirty-seven, Olivia,' he said slowly, as if she were a slow child, and suddenly his reasoning clicked. God, the man was impossible. Big, pedantic, tedious.

'You look older,' she said nastily, to teach him a lesson. 'All right, thirty-seven years, then. Are you telling me that your father included this room on the new house as a kind of memorial to his wife? I'll admit that I don't know your father very well, but he doesn't seem like a particularly sensitive or sentimental kind of man.'

To her shock Jordan grinned. But, instead of softening the hard angles of his face, somehow the humour merely emphasised them.

'No, but then my father barely looked at the plans. He rarely bothers to notice his physical surroundings anyway, so I had more or less a free hand. I included a studio because I saw it as an integral part of the character of this place, past, present and future. I wanted the house to be flexible enough to adapt to the changing needs of its inhabitants...'

'And you thought your father might take up painting in his retirement?' Olivia guessed, tongue-in-cheek. 'From what I hear he's taken up *business* in his retirement.'

'Actually I was referring to myself,' he said smoothly, acknowledging her amusement with a tilt of his head.

Olivia imagined a brush clutched in one of those enormous battered fists and her smile became laughter, which she quickly suppressed when she saw the glint of something approaching anger in his strange eyes. Goodness, he *was* sensitive... She turned away to hide her amusement, and froze.

She had vaguely registered that there were some art works hanging on the long fourth wall, facing the tall windows, but she hadn't realised what they were. She stiffened.

The Jester was staring her square in the face, mocking her with his distorted leer. Her heart began to skip irregularly. Sweat formed on her palms.

Her eyes slipped blankly beyond to focus on the works by Steven Foscoe and John Ferris, one a huge, sculptured relief in copper and leather and the other a sprawling triptych that showed the artist's exuberant mastery of his chosen medium. Olivia felt a debilitating pang of familiar self-doubt.

'Impressive, isn't it?' Jordan murmured, moving up beside her.

He was looking at the Foscoe. Was that his preference? Not that it mattered, Olivia told herself as she murmured her agreement.

Jordan moved along the triptych, which took up fully one quarter of the smooth white wall. The work represented a microcosm of city life at night, a complex series of pale blue and white calligraphic lines against a murky, smoky background. It was almost an abstract, but not quite. Olivia liked it enormously and said so.

Jordan echoed her opinion, in the careful manner of a man who was exercising some restraint. Perhaps he didn't really appreciate what he was seeing but was trying to impress Olivia with his understanding of art. Olivia suddenly couldn't bear to stand there watching, waiting as he studied her work and tried to come up with some meaningless compliment. *The Jester* looked coarsely unfinished lined up alongside the other two. In her imagination Olivia could practically see the blood seeping down the wall from the bottom of the frame. She turned away, muttering about getting to work on preparing her canvas, but Jordan was not be distracted.

He was silent so long that she *had* to turn back, and it was a shock to discover him looking not at the painting, but at her stiff attitude of detachment.

'Are you proud of it?'

It was so unexpected that she blurted out the truth. 'No!'

'Then why submit it with your portfolio?'

She shrugged sullenly. The question was unanswerable in the present circumstances.

'Don't you like it?' The soft question, asked in that deep, penetrating voice, confirmed her opinion of his ignorance about art and artists.

'It's got nothing to do with *liking*,' she said with angry scorn. He must know that she didn't want to talk about it. He must know what it represented. He *must*. He had seen and heard what the review had done to her. He had been *there* . . . She wished she was wearing some of her scruffy old jeans so that she could hide her balled fists in the pockets. Ordinarily she would have been gnawing her fingernails by now but even that release was denied her. His silence drove her to babble evasively. 'To tell the truth I was astonished to even make the short-list. I thought the painting had just as much chance of losing me the commission as gaining it for me. The modern idiom turns off many people, especially the older generation...'

'But you still submitted it. That takes courage. My father respects that. And then there's his knighthood. He knows that in art controversy is king. Some of the greatest art works of history were reviled and vilified at their first showing. He's looking for something that will make as big a splash. As you point out, it has little to do with liking and everything to do with total impact.'

He turned back to the painting. 'There's no doubt that this one has the most overwhelming impact on the senses. And it has one important ingredient that the other two lack.'

Olivia refused to ask him to expand his remark when he paused; she was too unnerved by his air of clinical detachment.

'And what makes you qualified to play art critic?' she asked snidely.

He went very still, but his voice was even and measured as he replied coolly over his shoulder with the hackneyed catch-cry of the uninformed, 'I know what I like. That entitles me to have an opinion, at least.'

Like. There was that word again. Olivia could learn to hate it. It was pallid and frustratingly uninformative, yet redolent with possibilities. It could mean anything. 'And you *like* this?' Defensively she pre-empted the anticipated put-down, 'You must have very perverted tastes...'

'As perverted as the artist's?' He followed her defensive remark through to its brutal conclusion. Olivia hunched her shoulders in silence.

'Aren't you going to ask me what ingredient I think the painting has that makes it so compelling?'

Olivia's eyes were as sullen and opaque as a winter sea as she expressed her mute indifference to his opinions. 'No.'

'Passion.' He said it softly, with a quiet certainty that was infinitely threatening. How could he possibly understand what she didn't comprehend herself? How could he see things that she could not? 'Blazing, illuminating, inextinguishable passion. There's so much intensity of feeling there, it's like another physical dimension to the painting. It's alive...' The turn of his head caught her in the piercing spotlight of his regard. He seemed to be feeling cautiously for the words: 'I was afraid...I thought that your crisis might have inhibited you creatively, damaged your spirit. But then I saw this...and if the painting took my breath away——' the corner of his mouth twitched wryly '—meeting the artist again was even more of a shock. Not only were you intent on playing some frivolous man-woman games but at the same time you somehow didn't seem to *connect* with your painting, if you know what I mean. You were so cool, so charmingly confident when you presented it, the contrast between art and artist was, I think, one reason it had such a crashing initial impact. At first I thought you had done it deliberately in order to——'

He stopped abruptly, and Olivia prayed it wasn't because he had suddenly pin-pointed the reason for his unease. Unfortunately she did know exactly what he was trying to express. He was trying to reconcile dual personalities with the same woman. Of course Roz had no internal connection to the painting, her appreciation of it was purely artistic. All *her* passion was reserved for the theatre.

'Did it work, Olivia?'

'Did what work?' she asked warily, forewarned by his gentleness, the caress to precede the blow.

'The poisoned-paint job. Did you get all the hatred out of your system?'

She rocked on her heels, even though she was ready for it. 'I don't know what you're talking about.' She denied it automatically, pushing away his intimate knowledge of her deepest distress, but he was relentless.

'A man hurt you so you fought back with the best weapon you had. You don't need to be ashamed of your lust for revenge. It was a natural and very healthy response. And it worked. You simultaneously eviscerated and emasculated him with dazzling brilliance and now you've hung him up for public ridicule and contempt. Is it enough? Have you forgiven yourself yet?'

'Forgiven *myself*?' She hated him for knowing what was at the root of her shame, striking out with icy venom, 'Designing a house for your own amusement doesn't make you an art expert, Jordan. I don't need a bloody *farmer* to teach *me* the meaning of my own work. You may *think* you know something about art but you're flattering yourself if you imagine you have any special insight. That painting is just an interesting experiment in style...since my last experiment obviously didn't succeed. Why don't you stick to analysing your goats instead of trying to foist your glib pseudo-intellectual interpretations on to my work——?'

'You don't have to be afraid of me, Olivia.' He interrupted her venomous tirade with a gentleness that was terrifying. 'I haven't told anyone about what happened. And I won't. Everything that went on between us that day is and always will remain...our personal secret.'

And that was supposed to be reassuring? He had no idea how personal his secret was. Even Olivia herself wasn't privy to all she had told him.

He stepped closer. 'If *The Jester* is just an experiment in style, why does it seem to disturb you so much? I don't understand what's changed. You *were* proud of it when you first brought it down here. You enjoyed displaying the shock of the new you. It was proof you'd risen like a phoenix out of the ashes of defeat: stronger, brighter, more brilliant than before. What happened between then and now to bring your demons back?'

'Perhaps it's you!' she accused wildly. His hard, square jaw came up, the muscles of his face locking tautly into stoic lines, as if this time *he* was preparing to weather a blow, but Olivia fumbled the follow-through. 'Stronger, brighter, more brilliant'...the words were luminous with promise. Was that really what he thought of her? Or was it Roz who had won his approval? She struggled to regain the courage of her earlier outrage.

'You're the one who keeps dredging up the past. Why don't you stop poking and prying? You're trying to *presume* on a very flimsy acquaintanceship, and don't think I don't know why...!' Olivia paused on the implied threat, hoping he would take the hint.

'Oh? And why am I doing it?'

'To throw them off the scent!' The subject of his sexuality seemed infinitely safer than the painful self-examination he was forcing upon her, and she latched on to it gratefully.

His eyelids drooped, his whole body suddenly taking on a stillness that to Olivia suddenly appeared menacing. She nibbled nervously at her thumbnail until she shuddered at the taste. 'Throw who off what scent?'

'Your family. You don't want them to know.'

'Know what?'

His puzzled innocence was very well done, but Olivia remembered the way that he had forced her to accept his invitation to show her the studio. With a few well-chosen words he had dangled the spectre of humiliation over her head. True, he had since admitted that it was an empty threat and, strangely enough, she believed him, but he had not been above blackmailing her with her own needless fears. She suddenly wanted to punish him with some of his own rough medicine.

'I want you to know that I'll always consider it our *personal* secret...' she said with malicious kindness, adding truthfully, 'I don't believe in condemning people

for being different. In fact some of my best friends have
been gay——'

'Wha——?' His jaw sagged, as if the blow had come
from a totally unexpected direction. He must have been
counting on her blind self-absorption to work in his
favour.

'What you do in the privacy of your own home is up
to you,' she continued smoothly, 'but I warn you that
I won't be your public alibi. If you're afraid to tell people
you're gay, that's your problem. I'm not going to pretend
I'm having an affair with you just to get you off the
hook——'

'*What*?' The exclamation exploded out with the force
of a gunshot, nearly blasting off her ears.

'And that means no more hinting that there's anything between us——'

'What in the hell are you talking about? *I am not gay!*'

At that, Olivia had made her grievous mistake of con-
tradicting him and now she was paying the
consequences...

Given her weakened physical condition, and his incredible size, Olivia should have been terrified when
Jordan grabbed her and forced her mouth to his, his
jacket sliding unnoticed to pool around their feet.

She could feel the coiled strength in the thick arms
that wrapped across her back and in the powerful
shoulders that curved inwards, conforming his chest to
her trapped body, turning himself into a muscular prison
from which there was no escape. He was rock-hard all
over. Even his mouth was hard as it roughly broke her
lips apart and plundered the softness within. He was a
man of huge strength and obviously unafraid of using
it. So why wasn't *she* afraid?

That she didn't fight him in the first instant was due
to shock, and once that passed it was too late. Olivia
knew from the banked tension in his muscles that he was
waiting for her to struggle. He was prepared—no—*eager*
to demonstrate his ability, he wasn't actually physically

hurting her... quite the reverse, she was horrified to discover!

She closed her eyes and went limp, hoping to fake him out. It almost worked. His grip relaxed fractionally before it tightened again, his mouth slanting more fiercely against hers, his tongue plunging hotly into her mouth with such wicked intent that her eyes snapped open again. His were open, too, sultry and glowing as they studied her frantic expression, his tawny gaze far more of a threat than his physical assault. It was as if he could see inside her, see what the touch and taste and smell of him was doing to her. See the hunger that sliced through her control.

She tried to demand he let her go and he ate the words as they formed in her mouth, imitating the movements of her lips with mocking little bites that devoured her resistance as she realised that he had no intention of letting her go until she responded! She had assaulted his male ego and payment was being demanded in kind. Against his strength they both knew that she was helpless and he had proved too cunning to fall for trickery. She had no choice. Or so she told herself...

Olivia let the rush of fire in her blood consume the last vestige of reason. Her mouth opened helplessly under his and he consolidated his victory, roughly staking his claim inside her as one big, calloused hand splayed across the base of her spine, lifting her forward into the broad saddle of his hips. He stepped back and turned, backing her against the smooth wall, widening his stance so that he could fit her between his powerful thighs, holding her there until she was vividly aware of his heavy arousal. She felt her first tiny thrill of alarm, and stiffened, but Jordan had sensed her instinctive withdrawal and skilfully thwarted it. His mouth softened its ravaging attack, suckling at her with a sensual skill that had more to do with his own engrossing pleasure than calculated expertise. He dipped and tilted his hips, fitting himself even more tightly against the V of her body, rotating and

thrusting even as his thighs bunched and clenched around
hers, pressing her even more tightly close against his intimate invasion. He was deliberately teasing her with his
body, heatedly exploiting the differences between them.
His restraint became unbearably erotic as he moved
rhythmically and persistently against her until she began
to arch and blindly move in an echoing rhythm. He
shuddered and moaned his thick approval against her
swollen mouth, his rigid body suddenly quivering with
a new and dangerous tension. Dazedly Olivia realised
what was happening. He was making love to her through
her clothes. He wasn't just teasing now, and he wasn't
going to stop. Though they were both fully dressed, he
was driving them relentlessly towards sexual fulfilment.

'No!' She pushed at his rigid chest but he didn't budge,
only lifted his mouth a breath away from hers.

'Liar.' The word was so thickly slurred that it was
barely more than a groan but Olivia instantly understood. She turned her head, pressing her hot cheek
against the cool wall, evading the stunning truth.

'I believe you,' she whispered raggedly.

'What do you believe?' he murmured impatiently, ex-
ploring her averted jaw, more interested in recapturing
her suddenly elusive mouth than in conversation.

'That you're not gay.'

His lips froze against her flushed cheek, the restless
movements of his body stilling as her words sank into
his clouded brain. She felt a brief, thrusting pressure
from his chest against her sensitive breasts as he took a
long, shuddering breath. His arms withdrew, bracing instead against the wall on either side of her. Her hands
automatically pushed against his solid chest, even though
she knew it would be impossible to dislodge him until
he was ready to move. Above the open neck of his shirt
she could see the throb of his pulse at the base of his
throat, rapid and strong. His skin, fine-grained in spite
of the weathered tan, gleamed faintly with moisture. His

gaze, when it snared hers, was strangely shocked, the colour difference more pronounced than she had ever seen it. His left eye was almost totally gold.

'What in the hell happened?'

The hoarse demand sounded genuinely bewildered and Olivia had no answer. She was as confused as he was, shaken by the impact of his male sexuality and her own response.

'I ... you grabbed me,' she said shakily.

'That's not what I meant and you damned well know it.' The rough harshness in his deep voice sharpened into a lethal, cutting edge. 'Who's been giving you lessons?'

'Lessons?'

'You sure as hell didn't kiss me like that last time around. Do you get your kicks from blowing hot one moment and cool the next? That's a dangerous game, Olivia; I hope you're prepared for the consequences ...' The tawny gold mist across his left eye was clearing, chilling over with icy blue speculation as he watched her colour fluctuate wildly. The speculation took a wild leap of intuitive perception. His voice was deep and dissecting. 'Or maybe you only blow hot when your inhibitions are unstitched—when you're drunk or when you're caught off guard. Like now. Maybe even *you* haven't figured out what turns you on yet. Is that what I am to you, Olivia, another of your little experiments in *style* ...?'

Olivia was blushing hotly, mortified by his list of maybes. 'Don't be ridiculous. I told you—I ...' She hesitated. She had to be careful here, remembering what had set him off last time. 'I ... thought you were ...' she coughed '... you know ...'

'No, I don't know. And I don't understand why on earth, if you believed I was gay, you tried to seduce me. Did you feel sorry for me? Did you hope to "straighten" me out?' His humour was purely ironic. 'Or did you think I was safe to tease, because I wouldn't spoil your fun by responding——?'

'No!' Tried to seduce him? Was he talking about that night in her studio? What could she say in her defence? She couldn't tell him that it was *Roz* who had suggested he was gay. And how in the hell had her sister, who usually had an instinct about such things, made such a monumental mistake? 'Well, I—I suppose it was *because* you didn't respond that I...well...I just assumed...' She blundered into silence at his expression of amused contempt.

'I see...' He shifted his hands on the wall, and she felt a rush of hope that he was going to distance himself both physically and mentally from this excruciatingly awkward conversation. But he was only narrowing the splay of his arms, caging her more closely so that his braced wrists actually brushed her sides. A fraction higher and they would be pressing against the slight swell of her breasts. Now her arms were trapped outside his and she felt even more horribly vulnerable.

'So you consider yourself so utterly irresistible that any man who doesn't instantly succumb to your charms must be gay.' His words were so heavily laced with sarcasm that Olivia's fingers curled into his shirt, fighting the urge to dig viciously into his chest.

'*No!*' He was making her sound like an amoral egotist! 'It was just a combination of things...of something someone said and——'

'Who? A man?' He was quick to pursue the clue. 'The man who's been giving you kissing lessons——?'

'*No!* I mean—no one's been giving me lessons. It was nothing—just a passing remark I obviously misunderstood. I'm sorry. Look, Jordan, please can't we just forget all about this? I know I was wrong——' she protested desperately, avoiding his eyes, unconsciously kneading his chest in her anxiety. She was going to *kill* Roz...

'What makes you so certain now?' he murmured blandly.

Olivia went hot all over. 'You…I…you…you were…' She faltered, realising where she had stumbled in her wild embarrassment. He allowed the tiny, hectic pause to stretch endlessly until he took up the challenge in a tone that was suddenly rich and languid, redolent with male satisfaction.

'Yes, I was, wasn't I? Extravagantly so. But no more than you…' Another telling pause before he continued the creamy drawl that was like a satin whip, stinging her senses with tender strokes.

'You're sure you wouldn't like another demonstration of my—er—heterosexuality? Just to clear up any remaining doubts you might have. I could take my clothes off for you, if you like, Olivia, so you could *see* rather than just feel what you do to me…'

'Stop it!' Olivia knew that he was being deliberately provocative, but she couldn't help reacting to the illicit pictures he was painting in her mind. 'Don't you think you've had sufficient revenge?' she said stiffly.

'Not now I have the taste for it,' he murmured and her eyes went involuntarily to his mouth. It curved sensually, knowingly, and she tried once more to push him away. This time, to her surprise, she succeeded.

He was smiling. *Smiling*. And such a smile!

'If this is revenge then I know now why they call it sweet. Did I mention I have a very sweet tooth, Olivia?'

Away from his distracting heat Olivia found her courage returning, albeit in a childish form in response to his goad. 'Go suck a lemon!'

He deftly picked up her insult and turned it into a provocative compliment. 'Sweet and sour, yin and yang, contradictory yet complementary too. How well you sum up the dilemma of male-female relationships——'

'We don't have a relationship,' Olivia snapped.

'Not for want of trying,' he murmured wryly. He moved suddenly and Olivia, alert to his every breath, betrayed herself by leaping back. But he was just bending to pick up his discarded jacket. He grinned tauntingly.

She flushed and gritted her teeth. When he touched her cheek with a calloused finger she forced herself to stand staunchly unafraid.

'It's a marvel to me that you can still do that.' He smudged his rough thumb back and forth, as if the colour might rub off. 'I thought you were far too self-controlled to blush. You've seen me nude and not turned a hair, and here you are blushing at the mere *idea* of it. But then, last time there was nothing to get heated *about*, was there? You were just going through the motions and we were both disappointed.'

Olivia was beginning to get a very bad feeling that had nothing to do with the tingling of his touch. A *very* bad feeling. To her uncertain knowledge she had never seen this man nude. She didn't think it was an experience one would forget even in the throes of an alcohol-induced haze!

But before she had a chance to probe, the door of the studio swung open with such suddenness that it thumped against the wall.

'Your father is still waiting to see you, Jordan,' Beverly said, her whole demeanour one of suspicion, which was confirmed when she saw the way they were standing.'

'Let him wait.' Jordan dragged his thumb downwards, across Olivia's swollen mouth, before he slowly dropped his hand.

'Does it take this long for Miss Marlow to see a room?' The sarcasm was as pointed as it was ineffective. Jordan was still looking down at Olivia as if she were the only woman in the room... if not his life. His words were imbued with meaning as he murmured,

'No. It takes this long for me to show it to her.'

'I can see why.' Beverly's gaze roved with contempt over Olivia's ruffled appearance and stopped dead at her feet. Olivia looked down and discovered that somewhere along the line she had lost her shoes. They were lying by the wall, their abandoned state rather indicative of Olivia's own behaviour a few minutes before.

Olivia bent to refit them to her protesting feet, hoping Beverly would put her flush down to the exertion but in the interim the shoes seemed to have got even smaller. She was taken aback when Jordan knelt beside her.

'Here, Cinderella.' He took control of her foot, forcing her to lean on his shoulder, his large hand easily able to completely encircle her fine-boned ankle. He frowned at the force it took to twist the shoe on.

'You have pretty feet. You shouldn't ruin them for the sake of fashion.'

'They're too big,' she said defensively, having always compared herself to Roz.

'They're strong,' he said, fitting the other, 'like your hands. Would you cripple your hands by binding them too tightly? These shoes are a good size too small for you.'

'Half a size,' Olivia corrected involuntarily and tensed as he flicked her a searching look that held a hint of perplexity.

To her dismay instead of getting up he ran his palm up the back of her leg as far as her knee. An intimate caress that discovered an erogenous zone she didn't know she had. A tiny thrill quivered up her thighs, tightening her flanks. She stiffened and his fingers deliberately stroked again at the back of her knee.

'I never imagined that you would be prone to petty vanity,' he said softly. 'I would have thought that, as an artist, you would despise the hypocrisy of fashion, not to mention the way it's used by society to manipulate and restrict women's movements and behaviour.'

Like him. Olivia felt a frightening stab of empathetic recognition. Jordan's casual clothes, his brutal honesty, his calm refusal to kowtow to family pressures expressed a bone-deep confidence in his own strength. He didn't care what others thought of him because his self-respect was more important. He was invincible. Unassailable. Complete in himself. And somehow his casual arrogance triggered the dormant resilience of her own nature, a fierce desire to fight for what she wanted. To take on allcomers. She would fight him, his father, 'the Jester', the whole *world* if necessary to win back the part of her that she had lost.

'Don't get your hopes up, Miss Marlow, he's not on his knees to perform a gallantly traditional proposal.' Beverly's tone was mockingly bright. 'Jordan views marriage in the same light as he views a suit and tie— as a choke-collar of conformity. He thrives on eccentricity. Even so I must admit I never thought I'd see him grovelling at a woman's feet. It's usually the other way around, as you graphically demonstrated this afternoon, Miss Marlow, although your reasons were more—er— *visceral*, of course. Or perhaps, Jordan, you've discovered some new and exciting fetish . . . ?'

On the surface it was just the kind of light sexual banter that any two people who knew each other well would exchange but there was a tinge of prurient spite in Beverly's tone that made the back of Olivia's neck prickle. Jordan rose unhurriedly to his feet.

'It's no use trying to tell Olivia that I'm a womaniser, Beverly, because she won't believe you,' Jordan said, with a grave amusement that ruffled both women. For one awful moment Olivia thought that he was going to make a joke about her embarrassing mistake but it seemed that he wasn't out to score points. Could it be that he still loved his ex-fiancée? Was that why he was so forgiving of her bitter tongue, so tolerant of her rudeness, her blatant intrusion on his privacy? And were his frustrated feelings perhaps returned? Was Beverly regretting her change of allegiance?

'No?' Beverly gave Olivia a smile of polite commiseration. 'How terribly trusting of you, my dear. Trust is *so* important in a relationship, don't you think? I suppose he told you that the reason your hole-in-the-corner affair has to be kept secret from his father is solely for *your* benefit, so as not to compromise what little integrity you have left?' The drop of acid burned through the rigid mask of politeness, eating away the mock-concern.

'We are *not* having an affair——' Olivia cut in, furious with the perpetuation of that myth, particularly now that there seemed no rhyme or reason for it.

'Oh, dear, was I supposed to have pretended I didn't walk in on you two, romping naked in his bed . . . ?'

'In *his* bed?' Too late she realised her mistake. The shocked emphasis in her involuntary exclamation condemned her more surely than Jordan's damning silence. But—*his* bed? The only naked romp she had had with Jordan, such as it was, had been in hers!

'Well, technically I suppose it was really *Alun's* bed, since this is his house, but I don't think the semantics matter, do you? From your behaviour today I doubt that you confine your enthusiasm solely to the privacy of any *one* bedroom.'

The new insult passed completely over Olivia's head. *His* bed? His bed—*here* . . . ?

'*Oh—my—God*!' A queasy sensation burst hotly in her stomach. Her horrified gaze flew to Jordan's face. His rigid restraint confirmed the unthinkable. The queasiness congealed into a tight, hard, alien mass.

'No, I don't believe it . . .' Her appalled whisper was too thready for Beverly to pick up, but Jordan's hearing was acute, as was his awareness of the disproportionate shock that had made her sway beside him. Again Olivia felt the focus of the probing intelligence that she had badly underestimated.

She wanted to scream out her accusations but she knew there was only one person she could vent her rage of betrayal on.

Roz. Beautiful, confident, flirtatious Roz.

Her sister.

Jordan's lover!

CHAPTER FIVE

'I DON'T think you've quite got me around the eyes...'

Olivia gritted her teeth. 'I'm only blocking in at this point,' she explained for what seemed the hundredth time.

'There's no point in building on a mistake. And you need glasses, girl. You've made my forehead too narrow...'

Olivia had always made it a rule not to let her sitters observe the daily progression of a portrait. The creative process was too personal to allow their self-involvement to intrude on and blur her own vision. Unfortunately Alun Pendragon refused to recognise any rules except those set by himself, and short of physical force there had been no way to stop him getting his own way. The last three days had proved that his own way was a strait-jacket of photographic conformity. Under the guise of being 'helpful' he was doing a very good job of sabotage!

But Olivia would have the last laugh... oh, yes! As an exercise in dominance the old man had disdained to set foot on *her* ground. Here, for the sake of her sanity, she kowtowed, but in the studio she reigned treacherously supreme.

Olivia dipped her brush into the thinned paint with which she had been laying in the main shapes and basic areas of tone, and cheerfully added a little extra width to the forehead. Her patron grunted and walked away, disappointed once more by the ease of his victory.

Olivia wished she, too, could walk away. Not because of Alun Pendragon. Arrogant old men she could endure. It was arrogant *young* men who confounded her.

She had thought it would be a simple matter to avoid Jordan, until he had suddenly taken full advantage of

Beverly's standing invitation to dine. Only breakfast was blessedly free of his unsettling presence. Even though he behaved with the utmost restraint, bordering on total boredom, Olivia found him thoroughly disturbing. Those mismatched eyes seemed to watch her like a hawk, his silence forcing her to fend for herself against the chilled animosity of his father and his haughty ex-fiancée as they sought to goad him out of his calm detachment. Or was it a vulture ... big, hungry, unnervingly patient, letting the others take their small predatory bites out of the prey only because he knew that ultimately it would be his to scavenge?

The only saving grace was that Beverly, who had initially been deeply distrustful of the reason for Jordan's continued presence at the table, had had her doubts allayed by his cavalier attitude to his erstwhile lover. But even that had its down side. Last night Olivia had been horrified to hear Beverly suggest, when Jordan casually mentioned that the roof of his 'barn' was being lifted off and replaced with shingles, that he stay at the house until the work was completed. Thank goodness the prickly situation between Jordan and his father made his acceptance out of the question.

'No wonder you're taking so long. Half the time you just sit there with a mooning look on your face.' Olivia was jolted back to the present by the sullen growl. 'My son seems to be under the misapprehension that you're inspired but I haven't seen any sign of it——'

'Your *son*?' She understood that it was William Pendragon who had used his influence on her behalf.

Her inadvertent exclamation seemed to grimly amuse him. Once again she caught an echo of Jordan in the sharp blue eyes. 'I didn't get rich through sticking my head in the sand. He may not be the son I want but he's still my son. I know him better than he likes to think I do. Will doesn't know art from his elbow, so his enthusiasm on your behalf had to come from another source, and it surely wasn't his fiancée since Beverly doesn't seem to cotton on to you very much.'

That was such an outrageous piece of understatement that Olivia knew he was being deliberately provocative. She refused to share his amusement, however. 'Since you don't either, that makes it pretty surprising that I'm here at all,' she said tartly.

'Isn't it?' The thought seemed to amuse the old man even further, but he couldn't just leave it there. He shrugged loftily. 'I wanted the best person for the job. I'm not in the habit of cutting off my nose to spite my face——'

Olivia couldn't help it. This time she did laugh. 'No? And what do you call deliberately driving out your only son?'

She expected him to explode at her presumption but he merely glowered and growled, 'It wasn't deliberate. If he weren't so damned stubborn——'

'He wouldn't be your son. If he were as soft and malleable as you evidently wanted him to be I don't suppose you'd have much confidence in his leadership qualities, or any respect for his character,' she scoffed.

'Oh, I respect him all right,' Alun grumbled. 'I just think that he ought to pay a little respect to *me*. I am his father.'

Was that what he thought? That his adult son didn't respect him? Olivia could see that for a proud man it would be a bitter pill to swallow. Was that what this obsession for a knighthood was really about—respect? Was that why he took issue with every word out of his son's mouth?

He shot her a look under his eyebrows and seemed to assess her thoughtfulness before he suddenly reverted to his irascible self. 'Well, your time's up! I told you you shouldn't waste time mooning. I'm off to my club in Taupo. And you can't follow me there because women aren't allowed, even as guests!' He got spryly to his feet, pausing only long enough to watch her bristle furiously at his sexist boast before he swept majestically out.

Olivia muttered under her breath, tempted to throw her turpentine-soaked rag after his dapper grey head. Instead she marched over to the telephone, taking out her temper on the hapless instrument as she punched in a familiar number. Thanks to several abortive and increasingly desperate phone calls, she knew her elusive sister's routine intimately.

This time she adopted the high, breathy tone of a mutual friend and waited, a grim smile playing on her lips as Roz's flatmate trotted away to drag her unsuspecting sister out of bed.

'If you hang up on me, Roz, I'm going to call Hugh instead and tell him *everything*!' Their eldest brother's sternly lawyerish manner had been mellowed considerably by marriage and three babies in rapid succession, all blessed with their mother's happy, if rather accident-prone temperament, but Hugh could still be oppressively intimidating if he felt his siblings had behaved badly or offended against the letter of the law.

'You wouldn't——'

'Try me.'

'Uh—I've got a rehearsal——'

'Not until eleven. Did you sleep with him, Roz?'

'Him who?' came the weak reply.

'You know who!' Olivia exploded. 'Jordan!'

'Oh, him...no, of course I didn't!'

Olivia had always believed her sister was a brilliant actress. Now she knew it.

'Sorry, I phrased that wrong, didn't I? I should have said, "Did you have sex with him while you were here?"'

'*Olivia!*'

Roz's shock was extremely satisfying. Within the family Olivia had always been considered the more prudish twin.

'Beverly told me she saw you naked in bed with him, so you may as well come clean——'

'*He* was naked, not me, and we were *on* the bed, not *in* it! Oh, damn, Livvy, I never meant you to find out! He was only there for the weekend, and he *said* he'd make sure that Beverly kept her mouth shut——'

'Well, he didn't and she didn't. Why in the hell did you tell me he was *gay*, for God's sake?'

'You didn't tell anyone *that*, did you?' Roz's horror was breathless and boundless.

'Only Jordan,' Olivia said grimly.

'Oh, my——' Roz made an odd choking noise. 'Wh— what did he say?'

Olivia blushed at the memory. 'What do you think?' she grated evasively.

Her sister obviously didn't dare to contemplate. 'Oh, God, I'm sorry... you asked and, well, I never did take too gracefully to failure.'

Olivia stilled. 'Failure?'

'It was all so *silly*. I only flirted because he kept giving me those intense, sexy looks... you know the kind I mean?' Olivia certainly did know. She shivered. 'So I thought, Well what's the harm——?'

'What's the *harm*?' repeated Olivia incredulously.

'All right, so I was thinking with my hormones,' admitted Roz hurriedly. 'I guess I got carried away with my role, but it all happened so *fast*... On the Saturday night, at dinner, we got quite chatty and he mentioned he had some interesting etchings in his room——'

'*Etchings*?' Olivia fairly shrieked the repetition.

'Well, daguerreotypes actually—and you know I've always been interested in photography. It wasn't a line or anything—he really did have them on his wall, Livvy, and they're incredibly interesting, you should take a look somet——'

'*Roz!*'

'OK, OK. So later on I sort of invited myself along to his room... just to take a look, of course, and I found that Jordan had just come out of the shower and, well... one thing led to another...' Olivia put a hand across her mouth, holding in the nausea, the roaring in her ears, almost obliterating her twin's next astonishing words '...except it didn't. I mean, after all those smouldering looks and meaningful *double entendres*...nothing!'

'*Nothing*?' Olivia took the hand from her mouth.

'Well, not exactly *nothing*. But when we kissed it just didn't feel right. No fireworks. It was rather an embarrassing let-down, really, after the build-up...'

Olivia remembered Jordan's words to her in the studio: 'You were just going through the motions and we were both disappointed.'

'And he was very kindly trying to tell me that I wasn't woman enough for him when that witch walked in and threw an I'm-so-shocked routine that you wouldn't believe, as if she were some delicate flower of Victorian womanhood, whereas we know she's got a hide of pure brass. And she never did explain what *she* was doing walking into his bedroom uninvited. Probably has the place bugged. If we really *had* been lovers I might have been really traumatised. I certainly wasn't going to give her the satisfaction of knowing what a fool I'd made of myself. It was all extremely humbling, which is why I was such a bitch when you mentioned him. So-o-o...if you've rung up to find out whether I have any prior claims the answer is a big, fat, sorry, no!'

Her flippancy was fresh fuel to Olivia's outrage.

'Roz!'

'Who are you talking to?'

Olivia was so shocked by the interruption that she slammed the receiver down and spun around, her guilty heart pounding in her throat. Jordan was standing only a few paces away. He had opened the door and closed it behind her without her hearing a sound.

'How dare you sneak up on me like that?'

He appeared unruffled by her guilty outrage. 'Perhaps they'll ring back. You didn't say goodbye...'

Olivia blanched again at the thought. 'Don't you have anything better to do than eavesdrop on other people's conversations?'

'I did knock but you must have been too involved in your conversation to hear me. Who were you talking to?'

'I...I...' You have a million acquaintances, Olivia. Pick one! 'It was...it was...'

'Your sister?'

'My sister?' she repeated stupidly, hoping her blankness would lie on her behalf.

'I thought you called her Roz. That would be your sister Rosalind. The actress.'

The last word she had said was 'Roz'. Please God let that be the only thing he *thought* he'd heard.

'Yes,' she admitted reluctantly, absently testing her thumbnail with her teeth before she caught herself and snatched away the temptation.

'Your *twin* sister...'

'Fraternal twin,' she said sharply. 'That means we're not identical. In fact we're not very much alike at all...'

She was babbling but she couldn't help herself. He made her so nervous, standing there like that, staring at her with those curious eyes. He was dressed in worn denims and a black sweatshirt that had seen better days, and tooled leather boots that might have been elegant once but were now scratched and scuffed and comfortably battered under the low sheen of years of polish. He would take care of all his possessions, one corner of her frantically skittering mind realised. He was that kind of man. He didn't value things just because they were shiny and new. He would look for quality and service, comfort over outward appearances. He would look beneath the surface for the meaning of things.

'You don't have to assure me of your uniqueness, you're definitely one of a kind.' Olivia anxiously moistened her dry lips. 'You seem...uneasy. Do I make you nervous, Olivia?'

'Not you,' she said quickly. 'This house. It makes me feel paranoid.'

He smiled and she edged backwards. 'I know the feeling. It's not the house, it's the inhabitants. My father been giving you a hard time? Perhaps you could do with a break.'

She *would* break if he didn't go away. Her nerves were stretched to the limit. She had come to the painful conclusion that she wasn't cut out for intrigue. She was trying to think of a subtle way to get rid of him without challenging that formidable male ego when he moved, very quickly and lightly for such a big man, and suddenly she was no longer blocking his view of her canvas.

'My God!' It was only a soft exclamation but it spoke volumes.

Olivia flushed. 'It isn't finished yet——'

Jordan proved no more easily convinced than his father, but for different reasons. '*You* haven't even started. Why didn't you just hand him the brush, and be done with it?'

His insight stung her pride but she refused to let him see it. She didn't have to justify herself to *him*. 'I don't know what you mean,' she said evenly.

'Surely you have more faith in yourself than this?' He gestured at the canvas. The worst of it was that he wasn't being deliberately insulting or accusing. He sounded . . . disappointed. Olivia was shaken with a treacherous desire to explain, to redeem her art and her honour in his eyes.

'This is none of your business, Jordan——'

'You think not?' He looked from the indecisive painting to its creator. 'Olivia, he loves playing power games, don't let him——'

Olivia lifted her chin and her eyebrows and looked down her nose at him. She had seen her mother use the same imperious gesture on stage to crushing effect. 'I know what I'm doing.'

Jordan remained uncrushed. Although Olivia might have the words and moves down pat, she could never achieve the bone-deep coldness of a truly haughty woman. She was too sensitive and too sensual. Her marvellously expressive eyes would always betray her. Jordan had seen them in a startling variety of moods during their brief but bizarrely intense relationship—blank and despairing, recklessly passionate, dulled and defeated—but right now they were blazing with a smug defiance that betokened some secret victory over her ignorant foe. Despite the evidence on the canvas before him her spirit wasn't broken.

Jordan was careful not to let her see his possessive satisfaction, sharply reining back his instinctive urge to strike back, to force her into a confrontation that she would inevitably lose. That wasn't the way to handle Olivia. He would let her enjoy her illusion of security a little longer. Her imagined superiority would make her all the more vulnerable when he did strike. Before he was finished Jordan intended to smash the protective shell she clung to so desperately, and possess all the secrets that she was using to keep him at bay. One by one he would strip away the veils between them. In the end there would be complete honesty between them—or nothing at all... He wasn't a man to accept half-measures in anything, or offer them.

He shrugged, changing the subject as if it were of little importance. 'I'm going back to the farm to pack. Why don't you come with me for the ride?'

'Pack?' Her heart stopped. Perhaps he going on a long trip somewhere—preferably the Antarctic. No, the Arctic—that was even *further* away. 'Where are you going?'

'Coming,' he corrected her and her heart began to beat again. 'Here. I'm moving in until they've done my roof.'

Olivia sucked in a savage breath, fighting her strange sense of relief. 'But you *can't*! What about your father? He'll be *impossible*. He'll think you're giving in to him.'

'Like you, you mean?' His smile twisted cynically. 'It's kind of you to be concerned about my pride, but I assure you that I can be far more impossible than my father. He'll be under no illusions as to why I'm staying.'

'But——' She wrapped her arms around herself.

'If you protest much more I'll start to wonder if you're afraid of the temptation I represent. Would it put your mind at rest if I told you that this time I'll make sure that I lock my bedroom door?' he said gravely.

She turned his mockery back against him. 'I don't think that'll be necessary. I never seduce unwilling men ... I certainly wouldn't bother to try it *twice*.'

'It would be three times, actually,' he pointed out wickedly, 'but who's counting?'

Olivia went rigid. 'You, obviously!'

'Well, someone has to keep a proper score.'

'This is not a game!' she burst out hotly, struggling to control her over-reactions to everything he said and did.

'I know. Look how tense you are.' Jordan disconcerted her by letting the matter drop as he picked up her stiff, white-knuckled hand and unfolded her cramped fingers. The rough, calloused friction of his palm created instant heat at the point of contact. 'You definitely need some time off—you haven't even poked your nose outside since you arrived. Why don't I get Tracey to make us a picnic lunch? It's very beautiful country out my way, only half tamed ...'

Like him. She blinked, trying to fathom his motives. 'Why on earth would I want to spend the afternoon with you?' she asked with husky incredulity, pulling her hand with remarkable ease out of his.

He raised a thick, dark blond brow and tilted his shaggy head. 'Curiosity?'

'I'm not the least interested in anything about you,' she said raggedly.

'Well, then, consider the fact that my father and I will be out so that it'll only be you and Beverly lunching tête-à-tête on tripe.'

'Tripe?' Olivia blanched, as much at the idea of being the sole target of Beverly's attention as eating the lining of an animal's stomach.

'I believe Beverly ordered it specially,' Jordan told her, straight-faced.

I'll bet she did, thought Olivia darkly. She had made the mistake, at the beginning of her visit, of responding to Beverly's polite enquiry of her particular likes and dislikes. Since then most of the meals had seemed to be deliberately planned around the latter. Beverly must have been saving the tripe for an occasion when Olivia wouldn't be able to get away with only pretending to eat in order not to offend her touchy host or the pride of the cook. No doubt Tracey already thought, from the size of the snacks that Olivia ordered between meals in order to survive, that their current guest was either a glutton or a secret bulimia-sufferer!

'I've asked Tracey for some smoked salmon salad and marinated mussels, honeyed chicken-wings, pâté and soft cheeses to have with crusty bread rolls and boysenberry tartlets and plum shortcake to finish up.'

Olivia's mouth watered at the list. She was suddenly ravenous. All her absolute favourites encapsulated in one meal. It was too good to be true but her stomach didn't give a damn about Jordan's suspect motives. At least this way she had an excuse to accept his invitation without compromising her flat denial of interest.

'There's no obligation, but if you *do* decide to come I'll be out the front in twenty minutes. Wear something warm because it looks as if it could cloud over later...'

His casual withdrawal was the perfect psychological move. Left alone with visions of sugarplums dancing in her head, Olivia soon persuaded herself that she could handle Jordan Pendragon. Beverly was another matter, however, and, coward that she was, Olivia simply left a message with Melissa that she wouldn't be in for lunch.

Half an hour later, as she sat in the passenger seat of Jordan's four-wheel drive, she felt less assured of her ability to act cool. The vehicle was huge and red and shiny, all tyres and bull-bars. A typical piece of swaggering masculine overstatement, she had decided nervously as Jordan had boosted her with crude over-familiarity up to the high door. He had grinned at her outrage. Most men looked younger and more innocent when they laughed. Jordan looked a decade more dangerous!

Olivia decided to remain primly silent to demonstrate her disapproval. Unfortunately that didn't seem to bother Jordan. He sang, his deep, husky voice mingling in perfect harmony with the country singer on the radio who was whining about an unfaithful woman who had trampled on his heart and soul. She squirmed in her seat. Was there anything the man *couldn't* do well?

He drove north, around the lake shore towards Taupo, before pulling off on to a road that was only sealed for a few kilometres. After that Olivia learned to appreciate the practical benefits of shiny red symbols of macho virility. If they had been in a car she would have been shaken to bits.

Jordan slowed his speed and cast her rigid profile a brief glance.

'Stomach feeling OK?'

She had forced him to speak first but his concern put a crimp in Olivia's righteous satisfaction.

'Of course,' she said stiffly.

'So you're not normally bothered with travel sickness?'

He always seemed to see her at her absolute worst. 'No. I'm not a delicate little flower, you know,' she snipped.

His hard mouth twitched. Did she think he was too stupid to see beyond her fragile appearance? Her opinion of him was due for some serious re-assessment. 'Mmm,

I do know. More like a tangle of wild briar rose. But it takes more than thorns to discourage me, Olivia.'

'With a hide as thick as yours, I don't wonder,' she said acidly and he laughed. It rose deep and warm from his chest and swirled around the cab. It made her want to laugh, too...

They turned in at a farm gate that Olivia had to get out and open, then close behind them. Jordan looked at her flimsy canvas shoes when she struggled back into her seat. They were already saturated.

'Why didn't you put on some decent footwear? Surely you must have realised those would be worse than useless in the conditions?'

She knew his impatience was justified, and that made her snappish. 'Because this is as decent as I get. I'm an artist, not a farm labourer.'

'You were wearing sturdy shoes the day you arrived. Why didn't you use them?' he demanded.

His eye for detail was incredible, and threatening. She drew her mouth into a stubborn line, but incredibly he seemed to read her mind.

'Too tight.' It was more a statement than a question. He sighed. 'I have some boots up at the house that might do.'

'I doubt it. Nothing that belongs to you would ever fit me.' And she wouldn't want it to, her tone declared.

He didn't miss a beat. 'Oh, I don't know, darling,' he purred. 'I can think of something of mine that would fit you with exquisite snugness...'

The indecent suggestion came right out of left field, and to Olivia's dismay she felt an incipient blush. She shot him the filthy look his suggestive words invited. He was waiting for it, his foot still on the brake, his arms crossed on the steering-wheel as he leaned lazily forward so that he could see her face properly.

'I was talking about an old parka I grew out of when I was thirteen,' he said blandly, and watched her blush bloom into full flower. 'You might need a coat. It looks as if it could rain later.'

'Then we needn't bother with the picnic,' she said severely, furious with herself for falling into his trap.

Jordan threw the vehicle into gear and they began to bump forwards again, up the long, winding, rutted gravel driveway. 'Oh, I couldn't let you starve,' he murmured. 'Since it was partly the food that lured you here.'

The word 'lured' held spine-tingling connotations. '*Only* the food,' Olivia denied.

'As you say,' he agreed equably. Just then they crested a rise and Olivia sighted the 'rotting old cowshed' that Alun Pendragon had been so scathing about.

'Good heavens!'

Jordan pulled up on the flat grey square of cobblestones, bordered on two sides with mature trees, that formed a frame for the impressive structure.

'It's so...*big*,' Olivia said faintly as she jumped down from the cab before he could help her. The word 'cowshed' had conjured vague visions of a typical New Zealand milking shed—long, low and strictly utilitarian. This was more of a Dutch barn, fully two and a half storeys high, half roofed in long sheets of curving corrugated iron pock-marked with rusting holes. The rest of the roof was a skeleton of arching beams and trusses, semi-covered with a patchwork of tarpaulins. Squinting into the sun, Olivia could see two men, high up near the ridge, cutting and removing sections of iron, moving about on the narrow framework with a nonchalant disregard for their dizzying height that made her mouth go dry.

Hurriedly she lowered her sights. The huge double doors that faced on to the cobbled yard had been sealed and a smaller, man-sized door, a bleached slab that matched the weathered timber walls, had been inset into one side, giving the quirky impression of a box within a box, an asymmetrical juxtaposition of shapes that appealed to her eye for composition and hinted at the intriguing possibilities within.

'I'm a big man. I need a lot of space.' Jordan called out and waved to the men on the roof, who hardly paused in their labours. 'Will you come inside?'

'Is it safe with all that going on up top?' Olivia asked, hanging back, imagining one of those heavy beams plummeting down on her head.

He placed a hand in the centre of her back, guiding her towards the door. 'Yes, just messy, that's all. Don't worry, Olivia, I won't let anything happen to you.'

'It already has,' she muttered wryly, but he heard her.

'What has?'

You. But she couldn't say that. It would tell him that he had assumed an importance in her life that she refused to admit, even to herself. She shrugged. 'Things have been happening to me all my life.'

He didn't pursue his question, moving past her to open the barn door and usher her inside.

The interior was big but that was where any barn-like resemblance ended. It was also very light. Large, uneven-sized windows had been framed at irregular intervals into the east and west walls of the building, providing a clash of light that ignited millions of dancing motes of dust into a bright, thick mist of brilliant white which hung through the room like a veil, billowing with each tiny change in the air currents. The ceiling was also timber, and surprisingly low, given the space available, thick beams supporting the wide planks of honey-coloured wood. Raw plaster walls lined the outer walls and a series of interlocking, folding wooden screens divided up the interior space into manageable proportions. Like the front door, they were a deliberate assault on conventional, static composition, reminding Olivia of nothing more than the off-beat whimsy of a child's jigsaw. She could see that, by utilising the screens in different ways, the whole floor could be opened out into a single space, or closed off to provide a variety of private corners.

The kitchen area, a jumble of state-of-the-art appliances awaiting installation, in a sideways U-shape formed by polished wood bench-tops, looked out one of the east windows. There was little furniture but Olivia's imagination filled the gaps with colour and form.

At the far end, on the windowless south wall, a huge stone fireplace with a slab hearth dominated the eye and to the left of it a startling curved staircase vanished into the thick ceiling planks. The banister-rail was as thick as a man's arm and carved almost haphazardly, letting the warp of the wood-grain dictate the shape of the rail rather than the other way around. Even from the other end of the long room Olivia was enchanted.

As she stepped forward a hand stopped her.

'Here. Wear this.'

'This' was a small white filter-mask for her nose and mouth. Although he had a mask of his own, Jordan didn't follow her. He stood while she prowled. The Pendragon house was elegant, cool, a masterly piece of conception, but this...this was marvellous. 'Earthy' was the best word that Olivia could think of to describe it. She stroked the dusty banister, frankly envious.

A hand joined hers on the rail, thick and square. She looked up. Jordan's eyes above his mask were very blue and, for once, a matched pair. Suddenly the mask took on a sinister purpose. It hid that brutal jawline, the hard, sensual mouth and hawkish nose, the features that served as a constant, needful reminder of his innate toughness. It altered her perception of him. His eyes, seen separately, looked curiously young and eager, two words that she would never normally have associated with such an aggressively mature man.

'A friend who's a wood-turner did this for me.' He caressed the wood next to her fingers as gently as if he were caressing a woman's skin.

'You——' dust seemed to catch in Olivia's throat and she had to clear it firmly '—you seem to have a lot of useful friends...'

'You sound surprised. I make a good friend, Olivia, a very good friend. I was a friend to you once, before you decided that made us enemies ...'

It was the mask, she decided, that made his voice sound as warm as his deceptive eyes. She looked away, up... 'Can we see upstairs?'

Again he accepted the evasion. He was giving her so much room that she felt trapped! 'See, yes, but we can't actually go up there, not while they're working. The original barn had a loft but Doug took it out to install this floor.'

As they mounted the stairs, Jordan's body briefly blocked her way as he drew back the heavy canvas which stretched across the top of the staircase. Olivia could see that the timber of the ceiling was actually the floor-boards of the second storey, huge, thick slabs of wood that looked rock-solid. At the moment the upstairs was just an empty space, half open to the elements where the iron was in the process of being removed, and where window-frames had yet to be glassed in.

'I'm shingling because the iron makes a hell of a noise in the rain, especially when you're this close to it. Since I'm going to be sleeping up here, we're going to put extra insulation in the ceiling for warmth and soundproofing, although we're keeping the natural curve of the roof-line for the interior. The skylights are going to curve on either side of the ridge-line up there, right above the bed. I want to see the sky at night, to lie here earth-bound and reach for the stars in my imagination.'

It struck such a chord that Olivia began to back down the stairs. 'Goodness, I never knew you farmers were so poetic,' she said flippantly.

'There's a lot you don't know about me, Olivia. Primarily, I think, because you're afraid to find out.'

She was debating how to make her denial sound believable when a bluff, square man in a grimy checked shirt and jeans hailed Jordan from the doorway with a query. Olivia joined them outside and was introduced

to the builder but in spite of his good humour she could
see from the anxious looks he was casting at the low-
ering sky that social conversation was the last thing on
Doug Chanter's mind. Soon the two men were deep in
consultation over technical drawings which the builder
unrolled across the bonnet of his grimy jeep, and Olivia
decided to wander discreetly. She had seen neither hide
nor hair of a goat yet, and was curious to know whether
there was any stock in the fields she had glimpsed behind
the barn.

As she rounded the far corner she forgot about her
goat-hunt. At the rear of the building was a square, windowless annex with a sloping roof which abutted the back
wall of the barn. There was a shiny padlock on the split-
stable door but it hung invitingly open.

Olivia pushed open the top half of the door, expecting
a dimly spooky interior. Instead she was surprised to see
a room diffused with light from the opaque perspex corrugated roofing. And what was in the room was even
more surprising. Blocks of stone, great and small,
trestles, sheets, tools and, in the centre of the concrete
floor, something that drew her through the lower door
and across the room; she winced as her soft soles con-
nected with the sharp chips that littered the floor.

It was slightly taller than she was. A thick, rectangular block of rough white stone, out of the top of
which emerged a clawing hand, an arm, the unmistakable curve of a head. It was not smooth, the shape
still inhibited by the sharp striations of a chisel, but the
raw idea was there, growing out of the stone's rigid
natural conformity as the outer form was peeled away
by the sculptor's vision. It was barely started and yet
Olivia could already sense the power in the slow process
of being unleashed, recognise the brilliant talent of the
hand that had guided the chisel. It was the same hand
that had formed the small stone carving which a remorseful Roz had paid so dearly for. A talent that Olivia
had admired to the point of reverence for years. She

turned slowly, seeing the other shapes, finished and unfinished, that lined the shambolic room, confirming the
incredible, the impossible. At the end of her three-
hundred-and-sixty degree sweep she saw another shape,
not made of stone, outlined in the open doorway. Still
she resisted the evidence of her eyes and deepest instincts.

'Junius works here...' Her hands spread out helplessly. 'I...he—you let him use this as a studio?' Unknowingly her voice held an element of pleading, a sliver
of panic.

Jordan didn't answer. He didn't have to. He just
stepped into the room and—*belonged*...

There was only one door, and he...Jordan—*Junius*—
was blocking it. Olivia was suddenly stricken with a very
alien attack of extreme claustrophobia. The world folded
in on her. Black dots danced in front of her eyes and
she swayed, inviting the blissful release of
unconsciousness...

CHAPTER SIX

THE escape was ruthlessly denied her.

A hard hand grabbed Olivia's shoulder. Something damp and chill clapped against her throat, making her recoil, gasping.

She blinked, the black dots clearing from her vision. Jordan was pressing a grimy wet rag against her collarbone, trickling gritty coldness down the open neck of her blouse.

'Don't——' She put a hand around his thick wrist and pulled ineffectually.

'Swooning fit over?' His tone was mocking rather than concerned. 'Now you know why they talk about curiosity and cats. But you couldn't have avoided the truth forever...'

Did he think she had been *faking*? 'That's rich, coming from you!' she choked.

'Up until now you didn't *want* honesty from me,' he said brutally. 'You wanted your nice, safe misconceptions kept firmly in place. I never actively hid anything from you, Olivia. I just lived down to your expectations...'

The idea that she had somehow invited this was too much to bear! 'When you've made such a point of *not* meeting other people's expectations?' she grated scornfully. 'There were plenty of times the subject came up that you could have mentioned it——'

'My artistic achievements are not considered an appropriate subject in my father's house,' he said with a dryness so pronounced that his voice crackled. 'There was plenty of blood-letting before we settled on our armed truce. The farm is an acceptable focus for his frustration, although it would have pleased him if it had

96

been a failure. The fact that I've made a raging success of my life without trading on the Pendragon name sticks in his gullet...'

'A *raging* success? My, you are modest, aren't you?' Olivia didn't want to know about his struggles, the difficult choices thrust upon him by his talent. It made him too real, too attuned to her own heart and soul...

His eyes narrowed. 'Should I apologise for my talent, like you with that abomination of my father?'

'You don't know what you're——'

'Talking about?' His laugh was savagely humorous. 'Oh, no, you can't get away with that line any more. As an artist I can *demand* your due respect! You have two sculptures of mine in your studio... you may not have any love for me, but for my work you have much more than mere admiration——'

'Your work, yes,' Olivia hissed fiercely. She had no intention of telling him it was now *three*. 'But that has nothing to do with *you*——'

She flushed as he laughed again. They both knew that in a talent of his calibre the two were indivisible.

'Poor Olivia,' he purred. 'Now you have two talents to try and come to terms with, mine *and* yours. Why don't you just give in and admit that we're two of a kind? I could show you...' she flinched, but he was merely turning to touch a small block of stone resting on the bench beside him '... in here. You and I could be inside here. Think of it... *Soul mates*... a man and a woman, forming one from the waist down, the upper bodies separate but curving inwards, protecting the secrets of their hearts...' His hands were moving over the thick block as if he was feeling the words he spoke as a finished reality. Olivia swallowed a constriction in her throat, hypnotised by the caressing sensitivity of his touch on the hard stone. Now she saw the purpose of the blunt, square hands, the chalky texture of his palms, roughened by constant contact with stone, the cuts and calluses, the ruthlessly short nails, one of them bruised with dark colour from a mis-aimed blow. For a moment she knew she was utterly forgotten as his mind reached for a vision which she could only vaguely appreciate.

'If you're going to ask me to pose, forget it,' she said, deliberately shattering his mood.

He wrenched his gaze up from the stone. 'I wouldn't need you to. You forgot, I know your body fairly intimately, Olivia...'

'No more intimately than I know yours,' she pointed out acidly, glad for the bulwark of Roz's recent revelation.

'Ah, yes...' His head tilted back, lids drooping over narrowed eyes. 'I was forgetting. As I recall you were rather—er—vividly impressed with my physique...'

She would *not* blush. At that moment, if Roz had been handy, Olivia would have throttled her. 'I've seen just as impressive in life class,' she tossed off casually. 'And, as we both discovered, first impressions can be *very* deceptive...'

She had been unwise to goad him, but the temptation had been irresistible. After all, it had been Roz who had failed to turn him on, not Olivia.

'Oh, very,' Jordan agreed, moving away from his beloved stone, watching her edge nervously away. 'But then we all tend to wear a series of masks, don't we, Olivia? At least until we feel we can trust people enough to remove them. Believe me, I didn't mean you to find out like this. I intended to break it to you rather more gently. I hoped you'd understand my reasons. Sculpting is just something that I *have* to do to be happy—a compulsion, if you like. The act of creation is what satisfies me, not what comes after—I don't want or need public recognition for it, and thanks to the farm I can afford to indulge my eccentricity because I know all too well the damage that the publicity machine can do to a person... especially an artist.'

The ache of a remembered pain was in his voice, slipping under Olivia's guard.

'Like you, I possess a publicity value which has nothing to do with my work. You've always had your family's full support, they've helped you handle the distorting pressures of a famous surname. I've never had the support of mine. Even William is my best ally largely in his own interests. So my anonymity, my privacy is very precious to me——'

'So why are you telling me all this? Aren't you afraid I might leak the story?' Olivia asked stiffly.

'I trust you.' There was a small, fraught silence before he added softly, 'I've taken off one of my masks, Olivia...what about you?'

One of his masks? The idea that there were even more layers to Jordan's devastatingly complex personality was terrifying. Olivia felt a surge of her earlier panic, her hand absently clenching around a chisel as she turned.

'I'd rather you put that to its proper use.' He wrapped a big hand around hers and angled the blade away from his flat abdomen. 'You can if you like. If you'd like to experiment a while, I can find some things to do——'

'I don't think my ego is strong enough,' Olivia said, shying away from the image of herself working beside him. 'I'm afraid that I don't have your ability to find the heart of a block of stone.'

'You underestimate yourself...but then that seems to be rather a failing of yours.' He took the chisel out of her capable hand and got rid of it, holding her fingers against his chest, where she felt the strong, steady vibration of his heart. Was he comparing himself to a block of stone? How could one man be so many things? He had a physical presence that was almost crude in its impact, a contradictory, cold intelligence whose detachment at times verged on the cruel, and yet she now knew that he also was capable of exquisite sensitivity, creating beauty with the power of his mind and talent.

'Is it really so much of a shock, Olivia?'

'Yes. I...I had no idea——'

'That I was a kindred spirit?' His voice deepened. 'Liar. You were just afraid to look. Come—let me show you what I'm working on right now.' He didn't let her hand go, interlacing it with his as he drew her around the studio. At first Olivia barely listened to his explanations of his work in progress but soon, as he had known it would, her artistic curiosity conquered her chagrin and her tentative questions flowered into a passionate interest in his thoughts, his philosophies and his techniques. When he reached the block over which he had described *Soul mates* he stroked their entwined hands against it, drawing her knuckles gently down the sharp edge.

'You can't send inspiration away like a naughty child once it's come knocking. It's going to haunt me if I don't do it, Olivia. And it will be very, very beautiful, I promise you...'

At that moment, caught up in the magic of the mood, she would believe anything that deep gravelly voice told her... if she let herself. She tugged at his clasp, jerking her knuckles painfully against a jagged stone corner. Two tiny beads of blood formed on the pale, scraped skin.

'I'm sorry, I don't want to hurt you, Olivia...'

Why did she get the feeling he was apologising for more than just bruising her knuckles? He raised her hand to his mouth and kissed away the blood, the moist rasp of his tongue disturbingly intimate.

'Then take me back,' she said breathlessly. She needed time alone to rebuild her defences.

'We can never go back,' he said gently, 'only forward. Like inspiration, knowledge can't be denied. I can't pretend that I don't know you——'

'But you don't. We're practically strangers——'

'Are we?' His eyes were deep, hypnotic and intense as they snared hers. 'Strangers who have slept together, fought, cried, kissed, revealed our secrets...'

'No!' Something stirred dimly in her buried memory; that night in the studio when the brandy had destroyed her control she had wept for all that she thought she had lost and he . . . somehow he had shared her grief. Those lovely miscoloured eyes had glittered with moisture as he had held her in his arms, stroked and kissed her with a passionless tenderness, held his damp cheek against hers and rocked her with warmth.

He had cried! To share someone else's pain so freely and completely would demand an awesome amount of courage and inner strength. It was his strength that she had feared more than anything else, the incredible lure of it. She had been afraid of her desire to lean on him, to rely on that strength, to indulge her appalling mental weakness. So she had thrust him away . . .

'I'm not Gabriel, Olivia. I'm not going to use you to get to someone else——'

Olivia's toes curled in her soggy shoes. 'I knew you wouldn't be able to resist throwing that up at me,' she said raggedly.

'That was another reason I didn't tell you everything about myself. I wanted you to know me as a man *before* you knew me as an artist. So that there was no way you could confuse your feelings about my art with your feelings for me. Gabriel Post is one hell of an artist but then you're one hell of a woman.'

Olivia laughed rawly. 'Oh, sure—that's why he spent all his time with me looking over my shoulder.'

Her traumatic discovery that Gabriel had been secretly having an affair with Diego's mistress, and using Olivia as a cover for his activities, had been devastating enough. Worse was the cowardice that had led her to hide her guilty knowledge from her mentor.

When she had found out that the man whom *she* had introduced to Diego's closed circle of intimates, the man she loved, was betraying them both, she had felt partially responsible. She had been so selfishly wrapped up in her love that she had failed to see what was happening. He had made her no promises, Gabriel had said carelessly when she had confronted him. He had offered her friendship, advice, admiration, and a little light romance...that she had mistaken it for passionate love was not his fault. There was enough truth in his words to make her sick with shame.

Already suffering from a chronic fatigue that was sapping her strength and clouding her vision, Olivia had succumbed to homesickness and fled the scene of her despair—right into the stone wall of another ignominious failure...

'Weren't you looking over *his* shoulder?' Jordan shook her out of her bitter reflections. 'Didn't you say it was his paintings you first fell in love with? And then in your mind you created a man worthy of them, worthy to be loved? That he wasn't was *his* failure, not yours. There's no shame in seeking to love and be loved, Olivia; don't let a couple of negative experiences deny you that part of yourself...'

'You think you know everything about me, don't you?' said Olivia shakily.

'Oh, no.' He smiled grimly. 'Not yet. I'm sure we have a lot more to reveal to each other. I do know there are no other men in your life right now, and there's no other woman in mine—or men, as I've already assured you...'

Olivia refused to respond to his teasing. She pressed a hand against her stomach, which was feeling hard with tension.

'Hungry? So am I. Let's eat.'

It had happened again. Just when she felt wretchedly cornered he walked away, leaving her feeling strangely bereft, aching with a restless frustration.

Olivia followed him slowly back round to the vehicle, noting that the cloud was ever-thickening in the sky, although the sun still provided a warm buffer against the cold air sweeping down from the mountains. By the time she got there he had fetched a pair of roomy black gumboots from somewhere, which he waited impatiently for her to don. Then he draped an oilskin parka over her padded shoulders and assisted her, this time discreetly by the arm, into his 'macho-wagon'.

'Where are we going?' she asked tensely, as he gunned the engine.

'To see some of my money on the hoof,' he said with a grin. 'You know, goats have an illustrious history. They're probably one of the first animals to be domesticated by man...' He was very eloquent and extremely knowledgeable on the subject as they bumped further along the farm road, and he spoke with a genuine, fiery enthusiasm that Olivia secretly found amusing. She guessed that the earthiness of his home was a truer indication of his character than his wealthy family heritage. She found it hard to imagine him in a suit, in an office, running a huge corporation within the rigidly defined rules of commerce, and yet he had done that, too, evidently with the same flair with which he did everything else. But in the end his nature had triumphed. He had made his choice and his contentment with it was the bedrock of his strength.

'The poor public image of the goat today is largely because of its ancient associations with paganism. The goat horn was the supreme pagan symbol of male power and dominance——'

'No wonder you decided to breed them; it was the macho thing to do,' Olivia said tartly, to disguise her interest.

He laughed. 'It was the *practical* thing to do. This is a volcanic plateau. We're fairly high up and there's a lot of surface rock. The grazing leaves a lot to be desired. Goats are agile and adaptable and prolific. They're well-suited to this kind of land.'

'So do you sell them for meat and fleece or milk them or what?' asked Olivia.

Her interest was genuine and Jordan treated it as such, becoming quite technical. 'So up until now we've operated mainly as an Angora stud—Angora is the breed that produces mohair—but we're going into full fleece production now that we've bred up our stock to Grade-

One level, although we'll continue to provide stud services for other farmers.'

He drew up past a rocky outcrop and Olivia gasped in delight. The land, well protected by trees from the prevailing wind, rolled gently away from the rutted track where they had parked to reveal the rising foothills beyond and, more distantly, the shrouded mists where she knew Mt Ruapehu must be. On the other side of the wire fence was a small group of cropping animals and Olivia got down from her seat, fascinated.

'I thought they'd be woollier.' She had never thought of goats as haughty creatures, but the animal with impressively splayed horns which stared at her over a mouthful of hay looked extremely disdainful. Certainly it looked nothing like the roadside goats she was used to seeing, tough and rangy. Its coat was short but thick and surprisingly white, its beard long and immaculate.

'They were just shorn a month ago, and they'll be shorn again in the spring.' Jordan picked a tiny tuft of fleece off the fence-post and handed it to her. It was very white and felt lustrous and soft in her fingers.

'You can't tell the saleable quality just by feel, it has to be judged by a micron count. The whiter and finer the fibre the better, of course. Only about five per cent of the world clip is in the fine range and that's the market we're aiming at.'

'You keep saying "we"...?'

'My farm manager, Kevin Curtis, is in partnership with me. Since obviously I have other demands on my time, I need someone to oversee the day-to-day work.'

She looked sideways at him. 'So this raging success wasn't all entirely your own doing...'

'Initially it was. I only took Kevin on full time a few years ago, by which time I was already in the black,' Jordan replied evenly. 'But I enjoy having a partner, someone to share the losses and celebrate the victories with.'

He lifted the hamper out of the back of the vehicle and carried it past her.

'Where are we going to eat—with the goats?' Olivia asked dubiously.

'And upset my pampered bucks?' Jordan arched one mocking eyebrow. 'I wouldn't dream of stressing them out by subjecting them to our inexplicable human behaviour. Goats are very susceptible to stress, you know, and at current prices those animals are worth thousands...'

Olivia followed him over the soft rising ground, leaving her oilskin on top of his in the cab. The grass where Jordan spread a large blanket was long and formed a springy cushion underneath the woven blue square. As Olivia sat on it she appreciated the subtle shadings of colour that loosely interwove to form drifting patterns not unlike the changing colours of Lake Taupo in restless weather.

'Mohair, of course,' Jordan confirmed as she opened her mouth to ask.

'Yours?'

He unfolded a small starched white linen cloth to protect the blanket, on which he placed containers of food and plates. 'Mmm. Kevin's wife, Charmaine, is a weaver; she designed and made this herself.'

'The colours are beautiful...'

'That's another thing about mohair—it takes dyes well, and resists fading and soiling. Charmaine is making quite a name for herself as a weaver of wearable art. Having her associated with our operation is a good form of publicity for us. 'Wine?'

Olivia looked at the chilled bottle he was holding, rivulets of condensation running down the sides from the gold foil top. 'I think I'd better have something to eat first,' she said huskily. It was difficult enough to cope with her reaction to Jordan sober; tipsy, her track record didn't bear scrutiny.

'Help yourself.' Jordan tore at the foil and twisted at the wire that held the cork in. 'Fill a plate for me, too, would you?'

'What do you like?'

'Everything you do.' There was a hint of warmth in his voice but when Olivia gave him a wary look she could see no flirtation in his eyes, until he blandly added, 'Our taste-buds must be well attuned.'

Olivia suddenly remembered his male tongue, hot and hard in her mouth, thrusting past her resistance, forcing her to accept his distinctive taste and scent, the instant, explosive overload of her senses when she had succumbed to the drugging pleasure, and the sheer thrill of the moment when she had realised that *he* was out of control, that *she* could command *him* ...

Unknowingly her eyes had darkened to a murky green, a smoky sensuality that made Jordan's hand slip on the damp bottle. Her narrow face with its still fragilely prominent bone-structure seemed suddenly to flesh out, to soften and bloom like her tender mouth as she breathed a soundless sigh. The plate in front of her was piled with food but she wasn't eating. Her cheeks were faintly flushed and her fingers hovered nervously near the neat pearly teeth that showed through her softly parted lips. If she had shouted her thoughts to him she could not have been more explicit. She was thinking of the mating of their taste-buds ... of their bodies.

His thoughts pursued hers. He recalled the feel of her, the tiny, rough sounds that she had moaned into his mouth, the way she had fitted to him, tight and satisfying against his swollen loins, easing the hungry ache even as she violently intensified it. She would sheathe him just as tightly when he entered her. Her illness had made her thin but she wasn't weak and her thighs would lock around him strongly. Once she had caught his rhythm he wouldn't have to be gentle, she would match him thrust for urgent thrust, and glory in the carnal savagery of it ...

Jordan shifted uncomfortably, the response of his body disconcertingly swift and painfully intense. The slow seduction he had in mind was in jeopardy. He was hard and ready for her now. Too ready. He lifted his thigh to hide the constriction in his jeans. If she stared at him with that sultry, wondering expression much longer he was afraid that he would throw her on her back and satisfy her curiosity and his lust with all the frenzied finesse of one of his rutting bucks. He had already proved to his own chagrin that with Olivia he couldn't count on the normal modicum of detachment he usually brought to lovemaking. Once he put his hands on her all hell broke loose . . . or, rather, heaven.

For both their sakes he had to damned well learn to control himself and that meant controlling her, because for all her vocal hostility her physical resistance to his sexuality was practically nil. His touch aroused her. His kisses made her moan. With just a few words he could make her eyes hotly desire him. The knowledge ripped through him like a jolt of pure alcohol. Like alcohol it also loosened his inhibitions and impaired his judgement, threatening his integrity. Olivia was fighting her instincts because bitter experience had taught her to mistrust them. She feared what a relationship with him could do to her and her fears were unfortunately justified. Whatever the progress of events, he knew that eventually he would hurt her, but by the time that happened he hoped that she would be secure enough to accept that the pleasure of knowing him far outweighed the pain . . .

When Jordan handed her one of the brimming glasses Olivia realised that she hadn't eaten a bite. She accepted it with a slightly shaking hand and hurriedly stuffed a mussel into her mouth, savouring the taste of the spicy shellfish.

'I think you should at least take a sip,' Jordan teased her in grave amusement, 'rather than spill it on Charmaine's beautiful rug. I doubt that a few bubbles will turn you into a raving drunk.'

Olivia flushed and turned her head away, looking down at the silver stream which meandered through the small valley below them. The view from the small knoll was breath-taking but her eyes were too glazed with embarrassment to see it.

'I wasn't referring to that night, Olivia,' Jordan said quietly, after a still pause. 'I know what damage glandular fever can do, how it can impair the function of the liver and kidneys. It's fairly logical to assume that that's what happened to you. It was my fault rather than yours. I shouldn't have made you drink such a large brandy. But at the time I didn't realise that you were seriously ill, and I thought it was the quickest remedy for your shock.'

Olivia's eyes burned with the effort of not looking at him, refusing to excuse her shame. 'I was in a temper, I behaved appallingly. At the gallery I——' She shuddered to a stop. 'I can only thank God that the Press didn't get hold of it. I don't know how they didn't— there were several other people in there at the time and it would have made a nice juicy story for the jackals...'

Jordan could have told her, but that would involve him in explanations he was not ready to give. He picked up a soft roll from her plate and spread it with rich dark pâté and held it up temptingly to her tightly closed mouth. She took a half-hearted bite and it was delicious. She would have eaten the rest but he did so himself, drawing her attention to his lazy expression.

'Your whole system was in shock. Don't take it so seriously, Olivia. So you broke out and behaved like a spoiled prima donna; that's better than dangerously bottling it up the way you had been. From what I hear it's not totally unknown behaviour for your family. Isn't your brother Richard famous for throwing people across film sets?'

Olivia felt a reluctant smile burst upon her face. 'Things, not people, and he never hurts anyone. It's just letting off steam.'

'That's what you were doing. Actually it was all rather exciting——'

'*Exciting*?' Olivia was disconcerted.

Jordan grinned. 'I walked into that gallery off the street expecting the hushed elegance of an up-town establishment basking in gloom, and there you were, dressed like an urchin but striding about with the guts-and-gusto of an avenging Valkyrie, hunting for the next target to skewer with your scathing fury. I don't think the poor gallery-owner knew what had hit him. You had two paintings off the wall before he had the presence of mind to scream——'

'He *screamed* . . .?' Olivia murmured faintly, her humiliation fading in the warm shaft of amusement with which he coloured the incident. Perhaps her solitary brooding *had* blown it way out of proportion . . .

'Like a banshee. But a cringing banshee. You were a one-woman riot!'

'That's supposed to make me feel better?' asked Olivia with a reluctant smile.

'You slugged me in the jaw.'

'I *what*?' Her smile was wiped out in an instant.

He chuckled. 'I deserved it. I hit you first.'

'Oh, God!' Olivia pressed hands to her hot cheeks.

'I'd never hit a woman before. I thought you were going to cry. But you're nothing if not unexpected. You wound up and gave me a round-house right. My jaw snapped shut so hard I bit my lip. There was blood everywhere. *Then* you started to cry.'

'Jordan!' She was horrified. 'Are you all right?' Coming months after the event, her concern made him laugh, a deep, relaxed rumble in his chest.

'My brain's still singing,' he said truthfully.

'And you still took me home?' She was morbidly fascinated with his revelations.

'I needed somewhere to staunch the blood. And I was worried about you. When you worked through your wildness I knew you'd need someone to hold on to. I wanted it to be me.'

'I suppose you rapidly regretted it,' she muttered, fiddling with a forkful of smoked salmon salad.

'If I had I wouldn't have tried to come back and see you,' he pointed out gravely. 'It was you who appeared to have all the regrets.'

'I was so ashamed. I acted like a...a drunken sex maniac!' There, she had said it, punishing herself with her crudeness.

'You were extremely upset, but it wasn't until after I made you have that brandy that you began behaving really irrationally,' he said patiently. 'Even a stupid man couldn't have failed to make the connection and I flatter myself I'm not that. I don't know how much you remember——'

'Not much, thank God——'

'But enough to colour your whole attitude towards me. Let's get it over with, Olivia. You were aggressive and, yes, wanton, but you didn't shock or disgust me. You weren't crude, just sensual and extremely uninhibited. If I had accepted your invitation *I* would have been the one doing the degrading, not you. You had trusted me earlier with your confidences and with your seductive behaviour you were entrusting me with your honour. It was love you really wanted, not sex. My pride was as much at stake as your own...'

Olivia cringed as she remembered the way she had flung that pride viciously back in his teeth. When she had woken up she had accused *him* of trying to seduce *her*. No wonder he had finally lost his temper and stormed out when she had refused to listen to him!

She lifted her chin and met his gaze as steadily as she forced herself to say, 'I suppose I should thank you for not taking advantage of me when I was...vulnerable.' She hurriedly took a sip of wine, bracing herself to hear how easy he had found his self-imposed restraint.

His blue eyes narrowed, becoming heavy-lidded and sensual.

'Mmm. Don't be tempted to thank me too soon, Olivia...'

Bubbles caught in her throat. Olivia choked. He waited until she brought her coughing under control before he calmly served her more food and drink.

'Got to build your strength up,' he said, as she protested the quantities.

'If I eat all this I'll barely be able to move.' Still, she was unable to resist the delicious fare.

'There is that,' he murmured wickedly, closing his eyes and stretching out full length on the luxurious blanket, resting his empty wine glass on his chest, seeming to fall asleep and allowing Olivia the forbidden pleasure of studying him at leisure, trying to fathom his appeal to her senses. A stiff breeze had blown up by the time he stirred again and she quickly dropped her eyes, licking her fingers, and gazing ruefully at the remains of the lavish repast, most of which *she* had eaten.

'Peel me a grape, will you?' he murmured, without opening his eyes.

He sounded as if he wanted to be pampered, just like one of his expensive bucks. The words slipped out and he turned his head, his hard mouth curving provocatively.

'Their pampering is all for one purpose and surely you wouldn't condemn me to *that*, Olivia? A lifetime of command-performance sex with every pretty little doe who's trotted in front of me?' He rolled over on his side, enjoying her flustered confusion. 'Do you know why the bucks have to be kept in such prime condition?' he continued relentlessly. 'Because once they're released on the does their sexual drive takes precedence over everything else, even eating... and a buck is never satisfied. Left to his own devices, he's quite likely to kill himself. Do I look like a man who would enjoy long days of endless, mindless sex?'

'No, of course not!' she cried in horror as a tingling warmth swept through her body.

'Now, should I take that as a compliment, or an insult?' he wondered wickedly, and chuckled as she threw a half-eaten bread roll at him. She was trying to think of something sufficiently cutting to take the smug grin off his face when a fat, heavy droplet spattered on to her nose. She looked up. The grey sky had become thunderously black.

'I think it's going to——'

It was as though a tap had been turned on in the heavens. Cold, hard rain suddenly fell like a solid sheet, joining earth to sky. Olivia leapt to her feet, gasping, and hurriedly began to thrust the remains of the picnic back into the hamper. Jordan grabbed her arm, hefting the heavy basket under one arm and sweeping up the blanket with the other.

They were both completely soaked by the time they made the shelter of the vehicle. Olivia was breathless, laughing with a crazy exhilaration as she ignored Jordan's orders and helped him heave the heavily wet hamper through the rear doors, climbing in after it, collapsing on the coarse carpet which had replaced the removable back seats. Even the goats had disappeared into the small, movable wooden shelters that marched under the shelter trees, Olivia noticed through the steamy windows.

Her padded jacket had been unzipped during the dash and the lining had become so saturated that it dragged heavily at her shoulders. Olivia peeled it off and accepted gratefully the large towel which Jordan handed her from one of the side-pockets. She knelt, mopping at her wet face and throat as he crouched beside her, waiting his turn. She had her arms raised, squeezing the moisture out of the rat's-tails of her hair when she registered Jordan's fixed attention. She looked down at herself. Since she had lost so much weight she had enjoyed the freedom of not needing artificial support, but her lack of a bra was now made glaringly obvious by the prominence of her breasts in her unconsciously provocative pose. Her chilled nipples were explicitly sculpted by the wet fabric, the flat aureolae surrounding the stiff peaks vivid, dark circles against the white cotton.

Olivia's mouth went dry. She found herself unable to move, frozen by a fearful sense of anticipation as Jordan slowly reached out...

CHAPTER SEVEN

JORDAN'S blunt fingers touched the drenched fabric at her waist.

'Take it off.'

'What?' Olivia's throat was so tight with emotion that the word came out in a rough whisper, scarcely heard above the roar of the rain on the metal roof.

'Your blouse. It's far too wet. Take it off.' His own voice was low and harsh.

'I...' He was still looking at her breasts, which were beginning to feel tight and hot in spite of the cold. Olivia could feel her pointed nipples hardening even further and she took a jerky breath. 'I'm not wearing anything underneath.'

'You can wear mine.' To her shock he pulled off his sweater and unbuttoned the shirt that had been hidden beneath it, stripping it off and holding it out to her. The roar in Olivia's ears wasn't just the rain, it was the tumult of her blood as her gaze roamed helplessly over his chest. His broad upper arms and ridged chest were hard and supple, muscular testament to the hours he spent in heavy physical labour. The fur that spread thickly between his flat male nipples was the colour of dark honey, arrowing down to his taut belly, where it flared again, just above the low-slung jeans. A few raindrops ran from his wet head down the hard brown throat and into the curling hair on his chest.

'Olivia?' She lowered her arms slowly and he said her name again, with a grim impatience that penetrated her sensual daze. '*Olivia*!'

She blinked. 'Yes?'

'Take it off...'

114

She swallowed hard; her cold hands went to the buttons at the bottom of her blouse in obedience to his hoarse demand. She fumbled slightly over the task and forced herself to slow down, conscious that her nervousness was turning a normally simple task into a provocative striptease. She was achingly aware of the growing tension in him as he watched each button drift from its anchor to widen the narrow pathway of bare skin. So she was stunned when Jordan tilted his head back, closing his eyes as she finally pulled the two halves of the blouse apart.

She faltered, uncertain. 'Jordan...?' The muscles of his chest had contracted with the movement, a shivering clench that rippled down his entire body.

'Have you done it yet?'

Was this his way of prolonging the terrifyingly delicious tension? With shaking hands Olivia pulled off the blouse and let it drop to the floor.

'Yes.' She knew that she was saying yes to so much more than his question.

'Good. Now put this on.'

He still had his eyes closed as he thrust his shirt at her.

'Your shirt?'

His jaw clenched. 'Yes, dammit. Put it on!'

She didn't know what game he was playing but she didn't think she liked it. She thrust her arms into the sleeves of his shirt, still warm from his body and male-scented.

'All right, I've got it on.'

He opened his eyes. She hadn't done up the buttons. He swore and crouched closer, performing the task for her with ruthless efficiency, although his fingers seemed to fumble as much as hers had. Now she was *certain* she didn't like this game!

'Jordan?' Unable to help herself, she reached out and lightly touched the flat brown nipple in its nest of honeyed curls. It contracted instantly against her fingertips. Jordan reared back as if she had thrust a hot poker through his chest, almost falling backwards in his haste to get away from her.

'For God's sake, woman!' To her chagrin he pulled his wet sweater back over his head.

He had buttoned the shirt right up to the collar and although it was loose around her slender neck Olivia suddenly felt unbearably constricted and felt for the top button.

He tapped her hand away, not gently. 'Leave it. I'm not going to have you going down with pneumonia and suffering a relapse.'

She looked down at herself, bewildered. The shirt was voluminous on her, billowing out to hide the contours of her breasts, which was just as well for she could still feel their betraying tightness. It was slowly getting through to her thick skull what had happened. She had made a fool of herself again. While she had been lost in a sexual fantasy he had been merely looking after her health. She wanted to sink through the floor. Instead, she scrambled hurriedly over into the front seat and stared out at the driving rain. It was his fault. How could she possibly relate to a man who blew hot and cold without rhyme or reason?

'Hadn't we better be going?' she asked thickly, when the silence from the back seat became too much for her.

Jordan was too big to copy her actions and there was a momentary swirl of cold, damp air as he got out the back door and sloshed around to the driver's side. He got in and started the engine, flicking on the heater and staring grimly at her averted profile.

'Olivia——'

'I hope they got the tarpaulins back on your roof on time—— '

'Olivia——'

'Goodness, look at the time.' Her watch-face was so fogged with condensation that she couldn't read it, but he wasn't to know that. 'Hadn't we better be getting back——?'

'*Olivia*!' His tentative attempt to get her attention became outright aggression.

'*What*?' she responded in kind, her face whipping round to challenge his for stony control.

'I don't know what you think just happened back there——'

'Nothing *happened*, Jordan.' No thanks to her! 'For goodness' sake, can we get going now?'

'Nothing happened because I wouldn't *let* it happen.' She couldn't believe he was spelling it out so cruelly.

'I said, it's all *right*. You don't have to assure me of your noble intentions——'

'There's nothing noble about my intentions, Olivia,' he said savagely. 'But I'm damned if I'm going to make love to you for the first time cold and wet in the back of a damned truck!'

Olivia's jaw dropped.

'Certain positions excepted, I don't like having my style cramped,' he said, taking particular pleasure in shocking the stony expression off her face. 'A man of my size enjoys sex better with plenty of leg-room.' Satisfied that he had her flabbergasted attention, Jordan retrieved the blanket, which, having been folded between the hamper and his chest, had escaped much of the downpour. He shook it out over the back seat and draped it over her.

'Another time you can show me your pretty breasts and I promise I won't close my eyes.'

She knew he was mocking her. 'Another time I may not feel like it!' she snapped, with what little dignity he had left her.

'Oh, Kitten.' It was a tender reproach, threaded with amusement. 'Did you think I didn't want to?'

He took her hand and drew it briefly down into his lap, laughing softly as she jerked it away again with a breathless squeak of embarrassment. Her palm tingled with the heat and hardness of him. Now she knew that when he referred to himself as a big man he wasn't only referring to his stature!

He didn't sing on the return journey, needing all his concentration to negotiate roads greased by the rain. He had only packed a single suitcase for his stay and they stopped briefly back at the barn to collect it, and drop off her borrowed gumboots. Jordan wouldn't let her put her ruined shoes back on, but gave her a thick pair of his own socks instead.

The downpour had eased by the time they got back, but it was still raining steadily. Jordan got out and opened her door for her, letting her struggle into the oilskin and slide off the seat, catching her by the waist just before her feet hit wet ground, and hefting her in his arms.

'Isn't this carrying your concern about my health a little *too* far?' she snapped at him as he carried her over the fine red gravel of the driveway.

'Sorry, but I don't want you ruining a good pair of tramping socks just to prove your independence.'

'Your——? Oh...' Chagrined, she looked down at her toes. She had forgotten that she was only wearing his thick, fleecy brown socks on her feet. She frowned up at his suspiciously tight jaw. It dipped and she saw confirmation of her suspicions in the amused blue eyes. She could have called him a liar but the argument was academic, since they'd already reached the door. He hitched her on to one hip while he used his key in the brass lock and nudged the door open.

Olivia only hoped that she would be able to slip up to her room and change before anybody saw her unusual outfit—particularly Beverly. The woman seemed to have a positive genius for being in the wrong place at the right time.

Today was no exception. As Jordan stepped over the threshold Beverly appeared at the top of the stairs. What did she have—an internal radar that homed in on intruders? Or was *Jordan* the gravitational force that she responded to?

As usual Beverly took immediate advantage of an opportunity to make Olivia feel like a grubby, graceless ragamuffin.

'This appears to be getting to be something of a habit, Jordan,' she drawled, descending upon them like an avenging angel. 'Has Olivia been sick again? My dear, you look quite dreadful, so very white and washed-out... How do you expect to finish Alun's portrait if you're prone to these fits of exhaustion at the slightest exertion?' Her eyes narrowed suddenly, as she noticed the shirt Olivia was wearing, and a very thin white line formed around her too-severe mouth.

'Perhaps it's because all your concentration is directed elsewhere? I'm sure Alun would be fascinated to know that as soon as his back is turned you forget about your supposed masterpiece and sneak off for a quick fling——'

Jordan set Olivia carefully back on her feet, a supporting hand behind her back steadying her as her wool-clad feet slipped slightly on the tiles. 'We were out at the farm and got caught in the storm.' His neutral, polite, unapologetic tone threw Beverly's open malice into ugly relief, which only seemed to enrage her more.

'I had no idea you were so interested in rural matters, Olivia. Next time you want to play tourist you'd better do it on your own time. And have the courtesy to make your excuses in person rather than leaving casual messages with the servants...'

'I'm sorry,' said Olivia meekly, following Jordan's lead. 'I hope the tripe wasn't wasted.'

'No indeed,' said Beverly smoothly. 'I told Tracey that she could serve it as your entrée for dinner tonight, since you missed out this afternoon. It's a regional speciality that you simply *must* try...'

Olivia heard a muffled sound that could have been a snicker that quickly changed into a cough as her head snapped around.

'Why don't you go up and change, Olivia, before you catch cold and have to miss out on our regional speciality?' Jordan told her, straight-faced. 'I'll just go out and bring in my bag...'

Olivia wasn't quite fast enough. She only made it to the first stair before Beverly caught her.

'You don't seem to be having much success at the moment, either personally or professionally, Olivia,' she said, any appearance of sympathy vanishing with her next words. 'Perhaps it's time that you reassessed your priorities and decided what you really want from your stay here—Jordan, or the Pendragon commission. Because I warn you, my dear, this is one case where you won't be able to have your cake and eat it too...'

'Are you *threatening* me?' Olivia wasn't really surprised. Beverly's whole attitude was a threat.

'Just a friendly warning, my dear. Alun wants his son back at any cost. After years of insisting that the two were incompatible, Alun's dangling the prospect of being in total control of a massive package of corporate art-funding under Jordan's nose to try and get him back into the company. If he accepts he could become New Zealand's most influential art patron. But Jordan will never come back on his father's terms.' Beverly stated it as a fact, with a bitter, vengeful satisfaction that was revealing.

Of course, the last thing that Beverly would want was for Jordan and his father to reconcile! That would threaten William's status and power, and through him her own. Thanks to Melissa's gossipy visits to the studio over the past few days, Olivia now knew that Beverly came from country aristocracy, a heritage-proud, land-rich but money-poor family, and one that Alun Pendragon wanted an alliance with. Marrying Jordan had been Beverly's ticket to the good life until Jordan had decided to step off the cosmopolitan money-go-round. Either to reward her for her strenuous efforts to dissuade Jordan from his defection, or perhaps to punish his son, Alun Pendragon had continued to flaunt Beverly as a favourite, asking her to act as his social hostess and ultimately brokering her recent engagement to his other heir.

Having moved into the Pendragon home, Beverly was perfectly placed to exacerbate the antagonism between father and son by subtly emphasising the points of conflict. Olivia was suddenly put in mind of a boa constrictor wrapping itself around its prey and suffocating it into insensibility before devouring it whole. Mmm, yes, that image suited Beverly exactly: sleek and reptilian, beautiful, cold-blooded and deadly.

'When Alun realises that his plan isn't going to work he's going to look around for someone to take the blame for his miscalculation. You, my dear, are already squarely in his sights.' If she called Olivia 'my dear' in that condescending nasal drawl once more Olivia was going to deck her!

'If Alun thinks you're trying to worm your way into Jordan's favour by taking his side then you're finished as far as this commission is concerned. Don't think that Jordan will give you any protection. He hasn't so far. And he won't. Jordan can be as single-minded and ruthless as his father when people threaten his independence. He's also a very secretive person. So don't fool yourself that you know him half as well as you imagine you do.'

Olivia unwisely allowed herself to succumb to the goad. 'If you're referring to the fact that he's Junius, I know. He showed me over his studio today.'

Beverly's hard eyes flickered, then steadied as she shrewdly assessed Olivia's words. 'You mean he volunteered—or did you just do a bit of snooping on your own and force his hand?'

Olivia's hand flexed at her side, but she controlled herself. She was *not* going to let Beverly drag her down to her own level.

When she remained silent Beverly persisted. 'You know, you don't have any special rapport with Jordan just because you're both artists. There's a world of difference between his kind of talent and your... shall we say valiant?... efforts. He felt sorry for you after all those truly *dreadful* reviews; that's why he asked William to put your name on his list, but after he first saw that painting you submitted, well...' her smile was filled with a twisted satisfaction '...he was so appalled that he tried to get your name withdrawn, but by then it was too late...'

'That's a lie!' said Olivia sharply, as she heard Jordan's lithe stride up the front steps. He had said the painting took his breath away... he had talked about passion, about impact. The old fear curdled in her stomach. Had his words been spoken out of pity?

'Is it? Why don't you ask him?' Beverly whirled and walked away, flipping Jordan a glitteringly tight smile as she passed him. Jordan's gaze flicked immediately up to Olivia's pale face and frozen stance.

'What did she say?' He dropped his bag and leapt up the stairs, halting just below her.

'Nothing.' Fiery rage smouldered beneath the frigid glare. 'Just being her usual pleasant self.'

'She must have said something to make you look like that.'

She couldn't hide from him, he wouldn't let her. So she lashed out. 'She told me that you originally put my name forward because you felt sorry for me——!' she began raggedly.

'In part.' He didn't spare her. 'But also because I knew your potential. I'm not unfamiliar with your earlier work... or some of the better stuff you did in France and New York. I told William that if you were well enough he couldn't *not* give you a chance——'

'Then why did you ask him to withdraw my name after you'd seen *The Jester*?' she burst out.

A shift of his shoulder revealed he had let out a small sigh. 'Is that what Beverly told you?'

'Was she lying?' Olivia countered.

'You should pity her, Olivia. I do. Nothing will ever be enough for her, she'll always be disappointed with what she takes out of life because she never gives in return...'

His evasion was duly noted. The brief flare of hope in Olivia's breast died. 'You hypocrite!' she said fiercely.

He laid a hand over her white-knuckled one on the banister, letting her feel the press of his superior strength. 'This is a little public for this conversation——'

'What—your lies are only for my private consumption?' she jeered rawly.

His palm hardened over her trapped hand. He leaned towards her, his voice hard and low. 'Don't play the self-righteous martyr with me, Olivia. I've had enough of it. I've been patient so far but I'm damned if I'll play by your rules to the end of the game.'

Game? Is that all this was to him? 'You mean you're willing to pretend to respect my work for as long as it takes to convince me to go to bed with you!' she accused wildly, the fiction she had struggled to maintain suddenly becoming confused with fact in her fraught mind. 'But since we've already failed on that score maybe you've got some other motive. Maybe your ego demanded a twisted kind of revenge. Maybe you needed to prove to yourself that you could have me anyway——'

He stopped her by the simple expedient of putting a rough hand across her mouth. 'And maybe I was just curious...'

He stared into her captive gaze above the fleshly mask, forcing her to acknowledge the brutal seriousness of his regard. Curiosity, was that all that had driven him? Olivia battled to keep the sick disappointment out of her eyes. He waited for a moment, then removed both hands with studied deliberation, setting her free as he snapped the trap shut around her.

'Curious to find out whether you were a better painter than your sister was a lover...?'

Olivia had already taken all the shocks she was capable of absorbing in one day. This, coming on top of all the others, was like a trigger, releasing a flood of adrenalin that surged to her head. She didn't feel weak, she didn't feel faint, she didn't feel guilty or remorseful. She felt mad. She felt ten feet tall and as strong as an ox.

She hit him.

He saw it coming but made no attempt to stop her. The force of her open hand across his cheek rocked his head sideways and he leaned with it, cushioning the impact of it with his body. By the time he had straightened she was gone, fleeing not up and away but down and past him, to the only place she felt safe: the studio.

She couldn't lock the door because it didn't possess one. But she didn't want to. She wanted him to follow her. She knew he would. He would want to pursue his advantage. While she...she wanted to rage at him, to hit him again, and again, and again... Olivia, the lifelong pacifist, wanted to pound him until he begged for mercy. How long had he known? From the beginning? From Roz's visit? What had given them away? What did it matter now? And he had accused *her* of game-playing! He was the master of the game! He was as bad as his father. She hoped that he *did* get sucked back into the corporation against his will and have all his hopes and dreams frustrated, the way he was frustrating hers.

Dreams. That was a laugh. She had only just started to have them again. After months of dreading the emptiness of sleep her nights had begun to be enriched once more by spontaneous images. Except they weren't the usual weird and wonderful insubstantial fantasies. Too often they seemed to involve *him*—thick and solid and

distractingly intrusive. Jordan had so thoroughly in-
vaded her consciousness that even the peace and privacy
of her lonely bed provided no escape from his disturbing
presence. And, as in reality, in her dreams he alterna-
tively taunted and touched her. Her feelings of hope-
lessness on awakening had been superseded by a
frightening feeling of helplessness, of inevitability...

She shuddered and cradled her stinging hand to her
chest. She looked down—at Jordan's shirt. Her skin felt
abraded by the soft linen. She wanted to tear it off, but
first she had to find a replacement. Fortunately she kept
a change of clothes in the studio and she hurriedly got
them out. Although the jeans and sweatshirt were old
and paint-spattered at least they were her own, and they
were dry. Out of necessity she left the socks on her and
pulled her wildly curling damp hair into a severe pony-
tail, securing it with a length of twine. She didn't have
to see her reflection in the long windows to know that
she was herself again, not a confused Olivia-Rosalind
compendium or a naïve fool who was intent on blindly
stumbling from one emotional débâcle straight into the
arms of another. Nice girls finished last. She had finally
managed to figure that out. From now on she was going
to be as rough and as tough as those who had the misfortune to cross her!

She paced, and when that didn't bring him storming
after her she packed and repacked all her tubes of paint.

When at last she realised that he wasn't coming she
felt hideously deprived. She couldn't cry—hardened
cynics didn't weep—so she did the only thing left: she
painted.

Everything she was feeling she poured into the canvas,
working with lightning speed alla prima—wet on wet, a
volatile technique she rarely used—producing a violence
of melting colours that perfectly satisfied her need to
outrage. It had no true form or pattern but it had an
abstract shape that transcended line. It pleased her. She
didn't hear the tentative knock and when Tracey slipped

into the room, an anxious expression on her homely face, Olivia gave her only an absent smile. The housekeeper respected her silence, merely observing her thoughtfully for a few moments, before bending to pick up the wet clothes from the floor and withdrawing. A few minutes later Melissa was there with a coffee-maker, which she set on the bench and plugged in.

Olivia finally stepped back and looked from the paint-soaked canvas in front of her to the leering *Jester* on the wall. Both were bold expressions of rage, both were effective in very different ways. For the first time she regarded the older painting with detachment, without cringing from the memories it evoked. It *was* good. Too good to hide away, or to hide away *from*. And she didn't have to any longer, for now she could see it as it was—a work of creation rather than of destruction. She could be proud of it, dammit, no matter what anyone else thought!

She put the wet canvas aside and placed another on the easel. Excitement filled her, blocking out everything else. It had been so easy! She had dabbled in abstract before but after her multi-media disaster she had lost her taste for experimentation, not to mention her confidence. Now, with angry, restless energy pouring through her veins, she felt capable of anything. Here there was no pressure to perform, just the intense desire to create a world where *her* desires, *her* needs were the only important ones.

She didn't notice him come in and for once she wasn't preternaturally aware of his presence. The sun was setting and the room was darkening but she hadn't noticed that either, crouching closer and closer to the canvas she was working on as she struggled to see the detail of what was flowing out of her brush.

It was only as she turned aside to wipe a palette-knife on a turpentine cloth that she saw him out of the corner of her eye, a bulky shadow leaning on the bench beside the now empty coffee-maker. After a glance she turned back and kept working, not faltering when the long narrow bank of lights overhead flicked on at his touch, or when she heard him moving around behind her. She painted until she knew that one more stroke on the canvas would collapse the integrity of the whole. He would see it too. If she continued he would know it was because she was afraid to face him. She threw her brush down and wiped her hands on the cloth. She took a deep breath, summoning her strength.

He wasn't even looking at her. He had walked across to a cloth-covered canvas in the corner.

'What's this?'

The prosaic opening took her off guard. But only momentarily. 'A portrait I'm working on.' She couldn't help the sharp reluctance that penetrated the curt phrase like a blade.

'May I look at it?'

For a moment she thought she'd misheard his meek request. Why did he even bother to ask? If he wanted to look, he would. But since he had, 'No.'

He was wearing black trousers and jacket over a white shirt, a monochrome attire that accentuated his golden blondness. He had showered and shaved while she had been sweating over her canvases. She could only see his face in quarter profile but she did see a muscle jerk along his sleek, freshly shaven jaw. He made no attempt to remove the cloth. 'Is it of me?'

Oh, the arrogance of him!' 'Whatever makes you think that?' She made her voice heavy with malicious amusement.

He shrugged black-sheathed shoulders, thrusting his hands in his pockets. Under the stark lights Olivia could see a streak of red along his half-turned cheekbone. My God, was he *blushing*?

'Well, it's not. *This* one is *you*!' She tilted one of the wet canvases in his direction, watching his back stiffen before he turned slowly, with such intense wariness that she was curious. What on earth did he expect, for goodness' sake?

He blinked at the razzle of flagrantly clashing hues.

'Colourful, aren't I?' he murmured. 'The blacks and blues are a particularly appropriate touch.' He lightly stroked his cheek and with a little jolt Olivia saw the faint swelling, the portent of future bruising. She wanted to apologise but the words would be a lie and there were already far too many lies between them.

'I'm normally a very non-violent person,' she said tightly. There, he could take that as an apology or not, as he chose.

'Except around me. I seem to arouse some fairly violent emotions in you. I like it.'

'Being slapped around?' Olivia was startled.

He gave her a wry look. 'No. The painting. Can I have it?'

'Sure.' Olivia viciously named an exorbitant fee. He didn't turn a hair.

'I'll write you a cheque tomorrow.'

Olivia felt cheated. She was spoiling for a fight and he was circling deliberately out of range. 'If you think you can buy me you've got another think coming!'

'Why should I need to buy you, Olivia, when we both know I can have you for free?'

She had left herself wide open for that one. Olivia went scarlet. She threw the cloth at him and he caught it against his shirt-front, leaving an aquamarine smudge against the formerly pristine silk.

'Ah, distraction but not denial. At least we're getting somewhere. Are you ready to talk now, Olivia? Or do we have to trade another round of insults before you feel comfortable enough to get down to the basics?'

Olivia realised how clever Jordan had been. He had deliberately stayed away until she had cooled down. He wanted answers that he knew he wouldn't have got from her former state of belligerence. He had probably even sent Tracey in to spy out the land!

'Does anyone else know?'

He didn't have to ask what. 'No. Do you want them to?'

She had been braced for the worst and he had knocked the props from under her with his answer. 'Surely what I want has nothing to do with it,' she said stiffly. 'How did you—how long have you known?'

'For certain? Only since this morning. Until then I simply doubted my own sanity. But when I heard you talking to your sister it all clicked into place.'

So he *had* been listening. Remembering the derogatory way she had referred to him, Olivia closed her eyes briefly.

He smiled sardonically at her expression. 'Among other things I discovered that it's true what they say about eavesdroppers. I had hoped that you might trust me enough to confess, particularly when the subject of my sins of omission came up, but since you didn't I felt entitled to watch you squirm a little. Your sister was very good, by the way. I must give her my compliments next time I see her.'

'Not good enough, obviously,' gritted Olivia, silently vowing there would never be a 'next time'. Let Roz find her own man...

'Good enough to convince everyone else. But everyone else isn't the man you cried secrets all over then tried to seduce. I think I've guessed some of it already, so why don't you tell me the rest?'

Olivia grimly obliged, not sparing herself in an attempt to deflect some of the blame from Roz, a detail that Jordan was quick to notice.

'Such commendable family loyalty,' he murmured when she stumbled into silence. 'Don't worry, Olivia, who better than I to appreciate your sister's persuasive charm? I was very wary at first. I didn't think you knew I was a Pendragon and I'd been afraid that you would react badly to my unexpected presence here but you— she—seemed totally unworried. I knew how ill you had been in the interim and I thought that perhaps you really had forgotten me but then you responded so... *enthusiastically* to my overtures that I decided that you merely preferred to forget your earlier embarrassment and concentrate on the physical attraction between us...' It was a pretty euphemism, but he wanted no misunderstandings.

'She was very sexy and I enjoyed flirting with her but as soon as I kissed her my desire died. Right up until that point I had been as excited as hell. It was most... disconcerting.' He looked at her and continued steadily, 'I don't usually take a woman just because she's willing, but that night I would have, if I hadn't sensed a sudden lack of enthusiasm that mirrored mine. I'd already rejected you once and to do it again after leading you on as I had would have been unforgivably brutal. So the fact that we didn't become lovers was the lady's choice, rather than mine, even though I was the one to cry halt. Her casual acceptance of my retreat confirmed my opinion, even as it added considerably to my male chagrin...'

Olivia swallowed, whipping up her family pride to smother the hot stab of jealousy. 'Roz isn't really promiscuous——'

He raised an eyebrow. 'As I said, I came on very strongly. She wouldn't have been a woman if she hadn't been flattered and intrigued by her dramatic effect on me.' Both eyebrows suddenly lowered. 'But either way she must have known she was putting you in an impossible position——'

'Roz is inclined to be—well, impulsive...'

'I guessed that much,' he said drily. 'Whereas you are exceedingly wary. You also blush like a virgin.' He paused, and much to his amusement she illustrated his point. This confrontation wasn't going at all as she had expected it to. He seemed oddly elated, rather than justifiably angry or condemning...

He gently removed the finger she had been unconsciously nibbling from her mouth. 'Your sister didn't seem to have a nerve in her confident body. She never blushed, not even when I walked into the room stark naked. I only have to *look* at you in a certain way and you pinken like a rose. You were skittish, you were hostile, playing dumb again for no reason. You were more sensual than sexy, your shoes didn't fit...' his voice dropped a full octave '...and kissing you was eating fire. No wonder I was curious.'

'You told William you didn't think I could handle the commission, even before I arrived.' Olivia clung to the painful wreckage of Beverly's malice.

'That's not what I said at all. I had what you might call a brief crisis of confidence. I had been wrong about you on one count and I wondered whether I had let my misjudged feelings unduly influence me on others. I decided not. If I made any kind of negative comment to Will when we were looking at *The Jester* it was my problem, not yours, that prompted it.'

She believed him. Not just because she understood his harsh, uncompromising attitude towards artistic honesty, but also because she had achieved a soaring belief in *herself*. His opinion was important to her, it was no use denying it, but it wasn't *vital* ...

'Now ... why don't you clean up and get ready for dinner?' He brushed ruefully at the turquoise smear down his front as he drew her attention to the lateness of the hour. 'I suppose I'd better come up, too, although I don't know if I have another white shirt ...'

For the first time Olivia realised that his dark clothing was formal dinner attire. The sleek clothes hadn't muted the raw, primitive energy that made such an impact on her senses. Sheathed in sophistication, he only seemed all the more untameable. It was not a reassuring thought.

'I'm really not very hungry ...'

He grinned, misunderstanding her reluctance. 'Don't worry, it won't be the tripe. William is back from

Wellington and he's brought back one or two guests who need to be impressed. I'm sure your sister made you pack something glamorous—her sense of style certainly annoyed the hell out of Beverly. Take my socks off and we'll go in shoulder-to-shoulder and knock everyone else's off!'

CHAPTER EIGHT

As PREDICTED, Olivia knocked their socks off all right, but for all the wrong reasons!

As soon as she walked into the dining-room with Jordan she knew that she was in trouble. The guests were two men, sharply dressed clones of the coolly sleek William, and their wives. All proved to be old friends of Beverly's, a fact reinforced by their cut-glass smiles and avidly sharp interest.

Jordan had swopped his stained shirt for a white silk polo-necked sweater that his father took instant exception to, with Olivia receiving the spill-over of his disapproval. When challenged on his unconventional attire, instead of offering the polite social lie that was justified in the awkward circumstances, Jordan had chosen to be stubbornly honest, murmuring a mildly censored version of the truth.

Everyone had immediately looked at Olivia.

She, attired in Roz's 'posh frock', which showed a great deal more cleavage than she was comfortable with, had blushed from the waist up. William, who she had thought was supposed to be Jordan's ally, albeit a passive one, had lifted his pointed gaze from her pink breasts and made a joking comment about the betraying marks on Jordan's face.

In reply Jordan had murmured something outrageous about running into a door.

'A five-fingered door, huh?' William mocked, displaying a set of white teeth that would do credit to *Jaws*. Jordan, damn him, had laughed and everyone had looked at Olivia again, salacious curiosity and disdain mingled in their expressions. Except for Alun Pendragon. Olivia happened to skate a look across at him and was

133

slightly shocked to find him looking almost amused, with an expression of wistful envy shadowing the ghost of his smile. When he caught Olivia watching him he managed a creditably bad-tempered scowl but the impression of a lurking vulnerability remained. Perhaps his envious amusement had been triggered by the novel idea of someone taking a heavy hand to his ungovernable son, or perhaps he had been wondering about the casual ease between two men whom he had done his level best to turn into bitter rivals.

Olivia was seated next to William at dinner, an arrangement which caused her great apprehension, but he proved a surprisingly entertaining companion. He was confident and voluble and although he was prone to a certain inflexibility of opinion she had to admit that he knew how to charm. He was perfectly courteous, not once repeating that sly leer at her gaping neckline, and she decided with relief that Roz's negative comments about him had been a typically impulsive throw-away remark.

After dinner the women left the men to the out-dated custom of port and cigars but Jordan once more created friction by declining the threat to his health and joining the women for coffee. He sat next to Olivia, helpfully plying her with cream and sugar and intimate little glances that were calculated to annoy. His mere presence was enough to alter the balance of power and instead of spending another long, boring evening fencing against Beverly's rapier-like malice, Olivia spent it trying to pretend a mental distance that it was increasingly impossible to achieve. She was actually relieved when the other men joined them and William again made a bee-line for her, thinking that she had better lobby as hard as she could for his favour now, before Beverly started pouring fresh poison in his ear. She might be doomed to failure but Olivia was determined to go down fighting!

He seemed very receptive to her ideas and she happily basked in the image of him as a perfect gentleman right up until the moment that Jordan had to rescue her from some very ungentlemanly suggestions next morning when she and William had inadvertently arrived first for breakfast.

'Hands off, Will, she's spoken for,' Jordan said, as he walked into the dining-room to find a flustered Olivia bailed up against the chafing-dishes, looking at his cousin as if he had just sprouted horns and a forked tail, which for all intents and purposes he had!

'She's not wearing a ring, cuz, that makes her fair game.' William didn't seem the least put off by being discovered in a mildly compromising situation. In the clear light of day William's charm revealed a cool calculation that lacked any real warmth. He didn't want *her*, he was just reacting because she was female and she was there. She was just an exercise for his obviously overactive libido. He *deserved* to end up with a woman like Beverly! Suddenly Olivia understood what 'going through the motions' really meant and was fiercely glad. If this slightly abstract detachment was all Jordan and Roz had shared then she had nothing to worry about.

'The only games she plays are with me, isn't that right, Livvy?' Jordan drawled, handing her the filled plate she had thought he was dishing up for himself.

Damned if she did, and damned if she didn't. Olivia didn't like feeling like the meat in a sandwich of male egos. She had given Jordan a speaking look as she sat down. His look had spoken right back, and very explicitly too. She had blushed and William had laughed, not unkindly, and Olivia had felt her dislike for him waver again. Perhaps she wouldn't wish him many years of unholy wedlock with the witch after all...

Jordan must have detected her confusion for when the others arrived to help themselves from the warming-dishes he sat down beside her and murmured, 'You don't have to worry about him, Olivia, Will can look after himself.'

'What do you mean?' She tried to move her chair further away, but Jordan just shifted his casual sprawl so that his thigh brushed her hip, and leaned so that his breath feathered her burning ear.

'I mean that he's not the charming cypher some people think. He's using Beverly in exactly the same way she's been using him—to consolidate power and curry favour. Sooner or later he's going to outmanoeuvre her. It's Beverly you should be feeling sympathy for, not William.'

Olivia stiffened. That was the second time he had exhibited compassion towards a woman who showed precious little to anyone else.

'Do you?' The scrambled eggs turned into tasteless lumps in her mouth that she swallowed hastily. She pushed the rest of her food away and played with her coffee-spoon. For all her unpleasant traits Beverly was still a beautiful woman. No one could choose whom they loved. Did Jordan turn the other cheek to Beverly's vicious taunts because he still, at some very basic level of his nature, loved her? Had they been lovers during their engagement? Did he suffer the torments of the damned, imagining her making love to his cousin? She didn't imagine that William felt the same torment, except that where the corporation was concerned he didn't seem to have a possessive bone in his body! To her horror Olivia discovered that she did—very much so...

Jordan sipped his coffee, which was as hot and black as sin, watching her over the rim of his cup, wondering what mysterious thoughts were making her mouth take on that brooding pout. She was wearing her hair down, the thick dark red waves a magnificent foil for her creamy pale skin. Because of that hair she would always attract male attention but, despite her thin skin and concealed temper, Jordan thought she was far from the conventional notion of a striking redhead. Dispassionately speaking, she wasn't really beautiful at all. She didn't make any attempt to project her femininity, as her sister unconsciously did, and she wasn't as graceful, but there was an earthy sensuality to her movements that had nothing to do with her appearance. It came from deep within, some central core of womanliness that Jordan found as irresistibly alluring as she evidently found it distressing. She had been devoting considerable stores of her depleted strength to repressing that very intrinsic part of her nature. Only when she cut loose from those conscious restraints did she come close to realising her full potential, as a woman and as an artist. He wondered how much longer it was going to take her to reach that conclusion herself. How much longer he could restrain his own masculine instinct to take the decision out of her hands. At times she made him feel unbelievably primitive.

At that moment her thick, dark eyelashes lifted to reveal irises the colour of a sullen, rain-washed sea flecked with dangerous hints of pure green. Suddenly he knew exactly what thoughts were going round in that bright, idiotic head. Primitive didn't even begin to describe the satisfaction that ripped through him.

'No need to be jealous, Kitten, I don't want her for myself,' he purred. 'Nor do I want her for Will, but that's not my decision to make. It's his and his alone. I would never apply the kind of emotional pressure I had to endure over my personal future. He knows my opinion; that's sufficient for both of us. I don't happen to think that Will is ready for marriage with *any* woman just yet...'

Olivia had never met a man who was. Why was it that Olivia's friends had lovers who were pleasant and ordinary and happily willing to share their mundane lives while she kept running into selfish brutes who were as emotionally free-spirited as they were exciting and unconventional? Perhaps it was that element of danger that attracted her, the irresistible lure of the flame to the hapless moth. No matter that she had had her wings severely singed; the average, pleasant, ordinary kind of man just didn't give off enough glow to distract her attention from her art.

A few minutes later, knowing full well it was madness to further expose the wings of her desire to Jordan's particularly brilliant fire, she had been falling in with his offer to take her around local scenic spots in the afternoons so that she might do some sketching. William was still directing flattering remarks her way and she told herself that perhaps it would be politic to make herself as scarce as possible until he and his guests flew back to corporate headquarters in Wellington. Beverly needed no extra cause for resentment. Alone she was formidable enough, but with her friends there to impress and to support her she would be utterly insufferable! There were only so many hours a day that Olivia could hide in the studio and, having no transport of her own, and loath to ask Alun Pendragon for any favours, Jordan provided the only escape.

That, afterwards, he gave the same reason for making the offer that she had given herself for accepting made it seem quite legitimate but in practice they spent more time tramping and talking than sitting and sketching, as none of the admittedly spectacular views he had chosen to show her had been accessible solely by vehicle. Having already practically turned her soul inside out for him once, there didn't seem much point in Olivia guarding her tongue, and since Jordan obviously had no intention of pretending an ignorance he didn't possess their conversations had roamed freely. Olivia only hoped that her growing fascination with him wasn't as evident in her manner as in her heart. Whereas with his family he exercised a cool restraint, out here, in the wilds of the countryside he loved, he was free and relaxed, sometimes shockingly frank and open where she would have expected reticence, and almost...*vulnerable*...yet in a completely masculine way. For some reason the thought of Jordan being as vulnerable to hurt as anyone else was strangely terrifying.

It was safer to think of him in his role as the rogue Pendragon, of such supreme self-confidence that he could stand alone against the rest of them. The artist who knew the cruel necessity of remaining true to himself and damn everyone else's opinion.

It was difficult, however, to maintain any pretence of disinterest when he threw out the lure of his intricate and awkward relationship with his family... and with Beverly. He had baited her with a few throw-away remarks during their first outing but on the second afternoon when he took her to the Taranaki Falls Jordan effectively ruined her concentration on anything but himself by becoming casually expansive in reply to her bold question as to why he and William could get on together whereas he and his father could not.

'Will and I went to the same boarding-school. We weren't particularly close friends because he was a few years behind me, but there was always a sense of kinship—particularly after his parents were killed in his senior year and my father took on his guardianship. We both spent most of our holidays working in some capacity for the corporation so it was as much a working relationship as anything else. I think even then Will sensed I was coasting... that our talents were complementary rather than competitive. At school I did well academically but I *loved* sports and art, while Will couldn't abide anything that got him sweaty or couldn't be controlled by logical thought processes...'

Olivia's charcoal pencil, which had been gradually slowing, stilled completely on the page as she eased back on her rocky perch at the edge of the boulder-ringed pool at the base of the Falls, the better to hear the deep drawl that was blurred by the muted roar of the twenty-metre waterfall.

'To his credit, my father treated us as equals but it was always with the knowledge that *I* was the one with the pre-selected destiny. If Will had chosen not to join Pendragon my father would have been disappointed, angry even, but he would have accepted it. I didn't have the luxury of choice.'

'But you did choose,' Olivia blurted out, swivelling completely so that her back was to the white curtain of water that was supposed to be her mind's focus.

'Not until much later. When I graduated from university I felt I owed it, not just to my father, but to myself, to find out whether running an empire was my true vocation. My interest in art at the time was purely peripheral. As it happens it took me ten years to realise that I might have the brains and instinct for business, but not the *heart*. William has that. It didn't satisfy me the way that I thought it would, the way that working with my hands always did. I think I was as surprised as everyone else when what started out as a relaxing hobby turned out to be the *real* challenge of my life. It took me a long time to come to terms with the fact that in failing my father I hadn't also failed myself. He still hasn't. Oh, I still feel a loyalty towards the corporation but no obligation to sacrifice my own dreams to its voracious demands. It's in good hands with Will. I think my father knows that, but he's too stubborn to admit it.'

'But he wants to. Isn't that what this is all about?' Olivia indicated the pad in her lap, wondering if what Beverly had told her was the truth or her own slanted version of it. 'Perhaps it's his way of reaching out...'

She thought she had made a mistake when his miscoloured eyes narrowed. 'Did he tell you that? Is he using you as a go-between, to say what his pride won't allow him to say to my face?'

'No, he didn't!' she said sharply. 'For two articulate adults you seem to have created a perfect form of noncommunication. You're both so suspicious of each other's motives that you can't take anything at face value. I'm just suggesting, as an impartial onlooker, that just because your view of your father hasn't changed doesn't mean that he has stayed the same...'

'Impartial?' Jordan taunted, studying her flushed face. 'Is that what you are, Olivia? And do your impartial observations tell you that he's entirely given up the idea of my trotting meekly back into the family fold?'

'Meek? You?' Olivia scoffed at the idea. 'Of course not! I'm sure he'll always hope you change your mind. But at least he's making an effort now to accept your choice. You don't have to reject it utterly out of hand simply because it's him making the offer. This art sponsorship idea has a merit of its own, you know. You could do it without compromising your high artistic ideals...or at least give it the support of your name...Junius, I mean...'

'He *has* taken you into his confidence, hasn't he?' Jordan murmured sardonically, a tawny flame flickering in his intrigued eyes.

'He didn't tell me, Beverly did,' Olivia said sourly.

'Ah...yes, Beverly...' Jordan's speculation turned to something more provocative. 'She was an impartial onlooker in her day, too, you know...'

Olivia looked down at her pad and began hurriedly sketching in the arch of a fern at the water's edge. When he prolonged the tantalising pause she applied such vicious pressure that the soft charcoal tip broke and he went on softly, 'Yes...she was everything my father approved of: impeccable pedigree, ambitious, beautiful, with all the proper respect for wealth and power——'

'She's a poisonous, selfish, snobbish bitch!' Olivia interrupted his paean of praise and then regretted her outburst when his mouth curved in a lazy smile. She turned her back on him to rummage in her art-box for the craft knife she used to sharpen her pencils.

'Ah, but then she was a lot younger, and so was I. I believed that beautiful things came in conveniently lovely packages. I was also arrogant enough to believe that she wanted me for myself. Little did I know that when I started to go through my change-of-life crisis she was reporting every move I made to my father. And there I was, wondering how he seemed to so perfectly anticipate and thwart my every attempt to withdraw gracefully from the corporation! When Beverly found she couldn't flatter me or use emotional blackmail or sex to convince me I ought to stay with the corporation she added her own ultimatum to my father's: shape up or lose her. I won!'

Olivia nearly sliced off the tip of her finger along with a thick curl of charcoal. *Sex*. Of course they had been lovers, she had made herself accept that. So why did the confirmation of the knowledge make her feel freshly murderous? 'Did you still love her?' Do you still love her? was how she wanted to phrase the question but didn't dare, for fear of how much it might reveal.

'What I loved was an illusion, but that didn't make the reality of betrayal any less bitter...I'm sure you know the feeling...'

Olivia's chin jerked up at the reference to her own less than successful love-life. He was still smiling but it was a kind of gentle smile that shocked her with its implied tenderness.

'I certainly don't entertain any warm feelings towards her now.' Olivia blushed faintly as her unspoken question was answered, loud and clear. 'She should have walked away back then—made her own life for herself, a career in business, perhaps, rather than nurturing this fixation on being the power behind the throne. Instead she clung rigidly to her own sense of betrayal and her conviction that the Pendragon family owed her a living. It wouldn't surprise me if she hadn't at some stage entertained hopes of my father marrying her, but he's too canny to let himself be pinned down. He finally came up trumps by more or less arranging this engagement with Will, but it's been a long wait and Beverly's too bitter to enjoy the fruits of belated victory...'

'She still wants you,' Olivia said, the stark statement an unconscious accusation.

'Only because she can't have me,' he said simply, without apology or arrogance. 'I'm not a man to her,

I'm a symbol of everything denied her. Her frustration makes her dangerous, especially now that she realises that she could lose Will, too—and her favour with my father if she's not very careful, or very clever. If she believes she can revenge herself on me indirectly, through you, she will. So be wary of any overtures from her, Olivia...'

Olivia was aware of the irony of the warning. She knew it wasn't Beverly that she had to be afraid of... it was herself.

She was very much afraid that she was falling in love with Jordan Pendragon.

Falling pretty well described the feeling, too. With Logan, and even with Gabriel, there had been a floating euphoria and a pretty rainbow brightness that had engendered a dazzling sense of self-satisfaction. With Jordan there was anything but satisfaction. Just this incredible sensation of plunging through time and space, every detail of the rushing world around her thrown into sharp relief by the dark, moody background of her uncertainties. No bright colours here, but dark blues and purples like the faded bruises on Jordan's face and an inky blackness beckoning, inviting her to lose herself in its hot, fathomless depths. But throwing herself into that welcoming black night would take a conscious act of faith that she was not ready for, might *never* be ready for...

Forewarned by her misgivings, it would have been sensible for her to re-arm her defences, but Olivia found that she was helpless against the impulsive urgings of her nature, and Jordan's relentless intent on proving his likeability. There was almost a trace of desperation about his purposeful intrusion on her life and, however disturbing and sometimes uncomfortable being with him was, Olivia had discovered that it was better than serenity without him! She wasn't totally in his thrall, however. A few days later Olivia stopped to take several stinging breaths of crisp mountain air watching, disgruntled, as Jordan forged on ahead up the gravel track. For every long single stride of his she had to take two. She waited for him to notice that she wasn't obediently trotting at his heels, and when he continued blithely on out of sight through the bush her mouth took on a stubborn set. She looked around and selected a good, solid-looking totara tree. She took off her padded jacket and tied it around her waist, feeling the sweat instantly cool on her heated skin. Then she leaned gratefully against the conveniently slanting trunk of the totara, to wait.

It was several minutes before Jordan reappeared around the curve in the track.

'What are you doing?'

'Resting.'

'We've only been walking for forty-five minutes.' Hands on hips, he regarded her with a frown. Even carrying the back-pack didn't slow him down. He wasn't even breathing hard!

'*You* were walking, *I* was jogging!'

Jordan had assured her that this tramp up the northern flank of Mt Tongariro to the Keretahi hot springs was well within her capabilities.

'All you had to do was ask,' he said mildly. He was humouring her and that only aggravated her more.

'You also said it was an easy walk for beginners. I *told* you I wasn't a very physical person.'

A smile tugged at his frown. 'I think that's debatable, don't you?' he murmured insinuatingly. He dropped his hands and strolled towards her, very much the cocky male. Olivia straightened hurriedly, just as two middle-aged, overweight women huffed into sight down the slope behind him, cameras slung around their mottled necks.

'Been up to the springs?' Jordan enquired pleasantly, standing aside for them to pass.

'Yes...we even dabbled our feet in the water, didn't we, Maria?' one of the women replied in a marked American accent.

'You didn't find the hike too strenuous?' Jordan smiled.

'Oh, no, it was worth every step. Once you get above the bush-line the view is spectacular. It's such a clear day, you can just about see forever.' The women laughed at the play on the song-title and paused for a few more pleasantries before setting off again.

Jordan watched them go and then raised his eyebrows at Olivia in silent challenge.

'Oh, all right!' she said sulkily as she joined him again on the track. 'I have been very ill recently, you know,' she reminded him sarcastically as they began to continue up the gentle rise.

'All the more reason why you should get plenty of fresh air and exercise.'

'I hate exercise.' She knew she was whining but she couldn't help it. She resented the ease with which he established his physical superiority. She couldn't fathom the man at all. One minute he was driving her mad by cosseting her as if the slightest chill would carry her off, the next he was harassing her like a maniac drill-sergeant. In the last three days she had walked more than she had in her whole life, but not for the world would she admit to Jordan that she felt any the better for it. Finding something to complain about had become a point of honour. It also took her mind off her weak-willed acquiescence to his every suggestion of an outing.

'It's good for you. You told me your doctor recommended building up your muscle-tone.'

'In gentle stages! I'm sure he didn't mean me to go racing up and down mountains...'

'We aren't racing. We're taking it slow and steady. I wouldn't have brought you if I'd thought you couldn't make it. Don't you trust me, Olivia?'

She sighed. 'Do I have a choice?' He was the keeper of all her secrets. If she couldn't trust him, who could she trust?

For once Jordan let her plod on in silence without trying to cajole her into revealing her thoughts, and it was with surprise that Olivia suddenly realised that they had broken out of the bush on to the higher slopes of the mountain, the track now winding through shoulder-height ti-trees, hebes, flax and bracken and other native scrub. A sign beside a look-out informed her that they had climbed to one thousand and twenty-five feet.

Olivia stopped, this time in sheer delight. Below, the forest curved over the lower slopes, flowing like dark green lava to the very edges of glittering Lake Taupo. Up above them blond tussock buttered the ridges and valleys that swept towards bare rock and the icy peak. Funnelling clouds of steam rose from a gash in the side of the mountain, the hot springs of their destination. The sky was a cloudless blue vault, the quiet as thick as clotted cream.

'I love coming up here,' Jordan murmured and Olivia tore her eyes away from the peaceful splendour to study him and to discover that, yes, he belonged here, dwarfed but not diminished by the grandeur of nature's gift. He looked at her, his eyes as warm as the sky. 'You've stopped complaining. Have I managed to take your breath away at last?'

He always did that! 'It's the altitude,' she said primly. 'I think I'm suffering from oxygen starvation.'

'Does your blood feel as if it's bubbling?' he grinned. 'That's not altitude, Kitten, that's exhilaration. Come on, it gets a lot more exhilarating than this!'

The track got steeper but Olivia could ignore the gentle ache in her legs as she enjoyed the view and the companionable silence as Jordan discreetly paced himself to her speed. As they climbed the scrub fell victim to the rain-shadow effect of the mountain and the harsh environment of the volcanic cone; in another half-hour they were wending their way through ankle-high tussock and mountain daisy and crawling hebes that were gradually being elbowed out by the introduced heather, which blushed over the land in spring and summer but was now dried red-brown by the threat of winter.

They could hear the sounds of the springs before they climbed into full sight of them—the human shouts and laughter that echoed in the crisp air. Olivia had seen thermal springs before but this one was a great deal bigger, the hot steam flowing hundreds of metres down a rocky crevice edged with black mud and red clay, the rocks themselves dyed white, yellow and red by the sulphurous water. Some of the pools where children now squealed in muddy glee were natural rock formations but others had been dammed by piles of loose stones, shifted and re-positioned no doubt thousands of times by successive bathers.

Jordan had suggested bringing swimsuits, but Olivia had balked, her imagination running riot with pictures of intimate little natural hot-tubs and sinful amounts of glistening raw muscle in tempting proximity to her own softer contours. Now she looked on regretfully, thinking that her self-consciousness appeared silly in view of the varying shapes and sizes of people innocently romping in the steamy rock-pools. She was cooling down rapidly after the walk and soon she would have to put her jacket back on.

'Changed your mind?' Jordan mocked her gently. 'I suppose you *could* go in in your underwear...'

Olivia's hand inadvertently fled to her chest and she pinkened, quickly diverting it to brush back a few curls that had escaped her pony-tail, hoping that Jordan would put her heightened colour down to the heat rising from the multi-coloured rocks around them.

Jordan clicked his tongue. 'You'll really have to start wearing a bra, Olivia,' he admonished wickedly. 'Apart from anything else you've started putting a little weight

back on. Soon you're going to find exercise uncomfortable if you don't have proper support——'

'I *am* wearing a bra!' Olivia snapped, a little louder
than she intended. She glanced around furtively, mortified that someone might have heard his teasing
comment. 'It's just I . . . it's very delicate lace and I don't
want to ruin it . . .'

A catlike smile slid across Jordan's face at her feeble
reply. 'You mean it's too sexy . . .' His eyes glinted with
intense male curiosity, mixed with amusement. 'Of
course you're right; veiled nudity is more provocative
than nakedness . . .'

He set down his slim-line pack and dug into it, pulling
out a very modest one-piece woman's swimsuit.

'I told you Melissa would happily lend you one,' he
said, tossing it over with a towel. 'She says she thinks it
should be the right size. Go behind those rocks up there
if you want to change.'

He pulled off his hiking boots and socks, undid his
belt and pulled down the zip of his dark trousers.

Olivia couldn't help standing and staring raptly as he
began sliding the trousers down over his broad hips.

'I'm already wearing mine,' he told her gravely.
'Disappointed?'

He laughed as she whipped around and scrambled up
to the safety of her changing-rock. The swimsuit was a
little loose but it fitted adequately where modesty really
mattered. Wrapping the towel round her shivering
shoulders, she made her barefooted way gingerly across
the warm rocks.

'Come on in, you'll soon warm up.' Jordan had found
one of the largest pools in a hip in the rock, dammed
on one side to raise the water level. He was already im-
mersed to the chest, his legs comfortably curving under
the overhang of the rock so that there was plenty of room
for Olivia to slide in beside him.

'Oh, that feels terrific!' she sighed as the heat seeped
beautifully into her bones, banishing her brief unease at

the strong sulphur smell. 'It's not dangerous here, is it? I mean, it's not going to suddenly erupt beneath us or anything...?'

'Let's put it this way, it's as safe as any thermal area is. We're OK as long as we don't wander past the danger-signs. In some places higher up the rock crust is so thin your foot would just go straight through into the boiling mud underneath. If this gets too hot we can move further down, where the air temperature has drawn off some of the heat off the water.'

'Mmm, no, I think it's perfect.' Olivia snuggled deeper into the pool. She was thankful that the water wasn't crystal-clear, so that she wasn't distracted by the big body lying beside her, and her reaction to his nearness was hidden by the grains of volcanic dust suspended in the water. It reminded her of the dust floating in Jordan's barn and her dreamy thoughts took her one step further as she traced the movements of a single, puffy cloud as it drifted past the peak, casting the fleeting shadow of its passage across the rocky ground. She imagined lying just like this, tucked beside him in his second-storey bed in a cosy cocoon of shared bodily warmth, staring up through the skylight at the endless sky, contemplating the delights made possible by all that unimpeded leg-room...

She should have blushed at her thoughts but she couldn't be bothered to summon one. The walk and the soak were working their sensual magic. Jordan was still talking, telling her something of the history of the turbulent volcanic region, how the land for New Zealand's first National Park had been gifted to the nation by a Maori paramount chief, of the Ngati Tuwharetoa tribe, in 1887. His gift for articulate expression made even the driest of facts sound fascinating. How well Jordan would get on with her wordsmith father. In fact, he would fit in far more naturally with her family than he did with his own...

She would have lain supine for hours but Jordan made her get out after a while to cool off, and fed her renewed appetite on mixed nuts and dried and fresh fruits and pure cold juice that he produced from his magical pack. In their rugged surroundings his raw masculinity seemed natural and unthreatening and Olivia found herself studying the flex and play of his muscles, and admiring the burnished sheen of his skin through the dark gold hair that covered his arms, legs and chest without trying to hide the fact that she found him a pleasure to look at. The swim-shorts he wore were modest compared to the racing briefs often worn by men of his impressive physique but Olivia completed her survey with the certain knowledge that his maleness, while not flaunted, was thoroughly stated.

After she had satisfied her hunger Olivia found a flat piece of rock and stretched out on her towel. 'I can't believe I'm sunbathing up a mountain at this time of year.'

'The climate up here is notoriously changeable, which is why I put in all the extra gear. While the sun's out you might feel hot but as soon as it disappears the temperature can drop radically. In fact we'd better not stay up here too much longer.' He glanced up at the sky, rather than his watch, assessing the angle of the sun.

'Mmm,' said Olivia dreamily as she closed her eyes against the yellow warmth of the sun. 'I don't suppose you have any chocolate in your bag of tricks?'

Jordan didn't reply, propping himself up against a rock as he watched her fall into a light doze. He could think of better ways to satisfy her craving for sweetness than with a surfeit of calories. In fact, he was so engrossed in his erotic thoughts that he let her rest longer than he should have, and then gave in to her pleas to have one more dip. By the time they got back into their clothes there was no one else left at the springs and clouds were rapidly thickening over the sun. Even in her extra sweater and hat and gloves Olivia could feel the chill.

With one last look at the sky Jordan led off—but in the opposite direction to what Olivia expected.

'What are you doing? Isn't it too late to go up any further?' she protested, stumbling in her borrowed hiking boots in a hurried attempt to waylay him.

'You see those clouds? They're going to dump on us in another hour or so, and, judging from the way the temperature's falling, it's going to be snow or sleet rather than rain. I don't fancy risking being exposed on the open slopes in that kind of weather and I doubt we could make the forest-line before it hits. There's a tramping hut just over that ridge—we can make it there in about half an hour.'

'And then what?' Olivia asked warily, totally at the mercy of his expertise.

'I've no intention of walking down this mountain in the pitch dark,' he said drily. 'Sunset's a few hours off but by the time this weather passes it'll be too late to attempt a descent. We're there for the night, at least. But we'll be warm and dry and have food and firewood. Don't look so worried, Olivia. The risk is quite minimal compared to the outrageous one that you took to get to Taupo in the first place!'

CHAPTER NINE

THERE were risks and then there were *risks*, Olivia decided over an hour later as she sat in front of a wood-burning stove sipping a mug of instant soup, watching Jordan string up their parkas and woollen trousers on a makeshift line above the heat. The front had moved in even more quickly than he had predicted, catching them in an icy shower just a few hundred metres short of the welcome refuge of the trampers' hut.

The building was spartan but equipped with all the essentials: stove, ample stacks of firewood, which Jordan said were toted up the mountain by helicopter, twenty bunks and a small store of emergency rations which they left intact, since Jordan kept a permanent cache of dried foods in a compartment of his pack. He had done a lot of tramping in the area, he told her, and was always prepared for the worst. He even had a slim-line torch which stood on one end like an electric candle, and enough spare batteries to last several hours. His knowledge and experience made her feel safe, even if her increasing awareness of their isolation did not.

It was almost completely dark now, the wind driving icy needles against the snugly reinforced windows, and unlikely that anyone else would be joining them. At least with so many beds to choose from she should be able to keep a respectable distance from temptation! The blanket that he had unearthed from a storage cupboard felt scratchy spread over her bare legs but at least it was warm and dry. Jordan wore his wrapped around his waist to free his movements.

The first thing he had done was light the stove and bring in enough firewood from the stack outside the door to last them the night. Wanting to take her mind off their situation, Olivia had got water from the small storage tank and heated up the soup, plain but nourishing and quite appetising when thickened with crushed crackers, while Jordan had checked the storage cupboards and produced the blankets. She would have been highly suspicious if his state of preparedness had run to the luxury of sleeping-bags!

Not that Jordan would *seek* to get himself stranded in her company, since his professed desire was still only disappointingly theoretical. In all the afternoons they had spent together he had never once seriously tried to seduce her. He had flirted, he had teased, he had made her laugh and blush but he had controlled any urge to touch or taste with apparent ease. He had acted like a friend rather than a potential lover and the restraint that had at first been intriguing and exciting was now beginning to feel depressingly like uninterest.

Perhaps he sensed the willingness underlying her wary reticence, and was bored by the anticipation of an easy victory? Olivia wished she was able to read him as easily as he seemed able to read her. She wished she had the experience and the confidence to knock down the barriers she had erected against him. Instead some archaic feminine instinct was holding her back, waiting for the dominant male to make the first move. Olivia had already discovered that she didn't handle rejection very well. Let *him* take the risk this time.

Risk. Olivia had already risked everything she had. She had fallen in love with a man of so many parts that she could hardly comprehend the whole: the broad-shouldered protector and the black-sheep son, the ruthless former businessman, the dedicated farmer, the illustrious talent, the perceptive intelligence and last, but by no means least, the physical *man* ...

The silence seemed to stretch on interminably as Jordan drank his soup and turned the gently steaming clothing. For dessert he produced a small chocolate bar, which he divided in half.

'So you did have some tucked away,' said Olivia, seizing on an innocuous topic.

'I always keep something in reserve for emergencies,' he said, revealing the intensely practical side of him that seemed so at odds with the exquisite flights of imagination that his art produced. 'We'll keep the other few bars for tomorrow.'

His deep voice sounded loud in the shrouded silence and she realised why. 'It's stopped raining.' Another gust of wind made the sturdy building creak but there was no accompanying rattle of icy drops.

'I am *not* taking you down this mountain tonight,' said Jordan curtly, crumpling the chocolate wrapper and throwing it into the firebox of the stove.

'I wasn't asking you to,' Olivia said, wondering at his swift annoyance. 'How long do you think we'll be here?'

'The mountain report was clear for both today and tomorrow, so I don't think this is anything more than a local squall. We should be able to get down first thing in the morning. You don't think I would have brought you up here if I thought the weather would close in, do you?'

'Of course not.' He was just impatiently reiterating what she already knew, so why should she feel slighted? A thought occurred to her. 'Won't everyone worry when we don't get back? What if they alert Search and Rescue?'

'They won't. I checked in at park headquarters, remember, and they know me well enough to predict what I would do if conditions changed for the worst. I doubt that my father would sanction calling a search until there was pretty good reason to suspect I was in trouble. More likely he'd send a helicopter up for a look-see before risking any embarrassing publicity. Either way nothing could happen until daylight...'

Plenty could happen by then, thought Olivia, and felt her skin go hot and prickly in a way that had nothing to do with the friction of the coarse blanket.

'I don't suppose you packed any cards in that survival kit of yours?' she said, desperately seeking distraction.

'No, but there is a rather dog-eared pack in the cupboard,' murmured Jordan, eyeing her pink face thoughtfully. He fetched it and fanned the cards out on the small wooden table between them, asking her mildly what she would like to play as he checked that there were none missing.

'Old Maid, perhaps?' His tawny eyes gleamed in the cunning torch-light.

'How about Donkey?' she shot tartly back. 'After all, if it weren't for one we wouldn't be stuck here. You *were* supposed to be the expert in local conditions, noticing little things like rain-clouds forming...'

'What about something more... demanding?' His smoothness acquired a tiny edge. 'Poker?'

He looked so smugly challenging that Olivia had said, 'Fine!' before she noticed the rapid skill of his shuffle. The cards rippled through his hands like silk.

'Why do I get the feeling I've been suckered?' asked Olivia as she picked up her cards and studied them warily, suddenly remembering why she rarely played. She hated losing. 'Four, please.'

Jordan flicked off her cards with lightning speed.

'How many are you taking?' she asked, looking glumly at the replacements for her discards, trying vainly to remember the rules of play.

'I'm sitting on what I've got.' He smiled at her brilliantly, which made her feel all the more sour.

'Yes... your big, fat——'

'Now, Olivia, don't be a sore loser——'

'I haven't lost yet!' She sat up straighter, glaring at her cards as if she could burn a few extra spots on them.

'Quite. So save your insults until you do. Now, what shall we use for money?'

'I am *not* playing strip poker!' Olivia yelped, with all the hasty outrage with which he had told her he was not taking her down the mountain at night.

'I wasn't asking you to,' he responded drolly. 'I don't need to resort to tacky stratagems to get women to take their clothes off for me. I usually just ask. We'll use these waterproof matches.'

He shared them out, and Olivia counted hers twice, waiting for her betraying blush to subside before she looked at him again. He was suspiciously poker-faced. With the same poker-face he then proceeded to beat her mercilessly until her little pile was reduced to a single, solitary match. More annoying still, every time she nibbled absently on a fingernail he tut-tutted, destroying her already flimsy concentration.

'I don't want to play this stupid game any more,' she said childishly, pushing the cards away with a sullen carelessness that sent several of them spinning to the floor.

'It's getting late anyway,' Jordan said graciously as he stooped to pick up her discards, revealing a startling amount of strong, hairy thigh as his blanket slipped. If his swim-shorts had been demure his silky European-style briefs were anything but. Olivia had automatically turned her back when he had slipped out of his wet trousers but it wasn't her fault she had found herself facing the rain-dashed window, complete with his daunting reflection... Talk about provocative semi-nudity—Jordan was it!

'I could have won if I played my cards as close to my chest as you do. You're a much better liar than I am,' she said doggedly, trying to whip up a defensive grudge.

Only the faintest hesitation tugged at his movements as he put the cards back where he had found them and fitted the conventional directional cone back on top of his torch. 'It's called bluffing, Olivia. And in the past couple of weeks I would say you'd had plenty of practise at it...'

No good throwing stones in *that* direction. 'I'm taking the top bunk by the window,' she announced, gathering her dignity around her, along with the trailing blanket, as she marched over to her prime location.

'It'll have to be the bottom. The top won't take the weight.'

'Don't be ridiculous. If *you* can carry me, this bunk certainly can. That's what it's built for, for goodness' sake!'

'If it were only you I'd agree. But I wouldn't want to risk our combined weight on it.'

Risk. That zinging word again.

He switched off the torch, the light swallowed along with her ability to speak. The glow from the stove was only just enough to indicate his general outline... big, bold, solidly male. She wasn't ready for this after all... She found her shocked tongue.

'Jordan——'

'There aren't enough blankets for us to sleep in separate beds, Olivia,' he cut across her wavering protest. 'We only have these two. Even with the stove going the temperature is going to be too low for comfort, especially in the early hours. If we want to sleep we're going to have to do it together...'

'Maybe I could just stay up——'

'Not if you want to walk down that mountain tomorrow. If the conditions aren't the best you'll need all your strength and stamina. Your choice, Olivia...'

Again a choice that was no choice! She knew what *she* wanted, but what did *he* want?

'It's not as if we hadn't done it before.'

Olivia winced. 'You would remind me of *that*——'

'I'm just reassuring you that it is possible for a man to hold a woman without succumbing to involuntary sexual responses.'

Is *that* what he thought it was? Just an involuntary sexual response?

'Olivia——?'

'I'm thinking!'

'Don't think. Just feel.' He was there, surrounding her with his warmth, enfolding her in his blanket and drawing her into his body. It was like being back in the liquid depths of the hot springs, with one vital difference. The springs had relaxed her, rather than wound her as tight as a bow-string. 'See? Shared body heat is the best defence against the cold. It's the logical thing to do, Olivia.'

'I...these bunks are pretty narrow. I...don't think there's room for two...'

'Let's see, shall we?' He was speaking and moving slowly, as if afraid of startling her. There was a dark rustling.

'W...what are you doing?'

'Taking off my jumper and shirt. It's skin that transfers heat, Livvy, not clothing. We can spread the sweaters on top of the blankets. Come on.' He took her blanket out of her nerveless fingers and spread half of it with his across the thin mattress on the bottom bunk. The slats creaked as he got in, lying on his side, the other half of the blankets draped over the top of him, ready to open to receive her.

So he was going to see her underwear after all, although perhaps only subliminally! The darkness gave Olivia the illusion of modesty as she quickly shed the rest of her clothes and clumsily spread them over the long shape of his body. She stubbed her toe moving around the end of the bunk and muttered a curse as she stopped to rub it.

'Stop procrastinating, Olivia, and get in.'

'I'm not procrastinating!' It *was* cold. A damp, unpleasant cold that slithered into the bones. She wavered.

'You're right, you *are* a poor liar.' His voice took on a musing note. 'You know, posed in silhouette against the stove like that, you remind me of that kitsch American painting of the nude woman bathing in the lake... *September Morn*, isn't it? Umph!'

Jordan let out a coughing grunt as Olivia slammed herself into the bed, wedging her back against his front with the help of a sharp elbow, and wrenching the covers tightly across her. The movement pulled him even more tightly against her and she let out a little gasp as his hairy arm came around her waist to fumble in front of her.

'Relax, I'm just tucking the blankets in. Lift your shoulder and hip so that I can slide the ends under you. That's right. See, now we're pretty well air-tight.'

Everything-else-tight, too. When Jordan had finished his tucking he didn't shift his arm away. It remained, snugly curved over her tense diaphragm. His legs, bent to fit the small bed, nudged up under her thighs. His breath was sweet and warm on her bare shoulder—and moist... Olivia stiffened.

'Relax.' He kissed the crease between her shoulder and neck again, his tongue moving against her skin. 'You taste of sulphur.'

'Then stop licking me,' Olivia said huskily.

'I didn't stay I didn't like it.' He did it again, a flickering rasp over her tingling nerves.

'Jordan——'

'Goodnight, Olivia.' He snuggled against her with a brief squeezing pressure that she felt right to her toes.

Goodnight? Olivia lay there, trying to gauge from the steady, rhythmic movement of the massive chest against her shoulder-blades whether he was actually falling asleep.

Relax! How could she when she was aware of every shifting cell in his body... and hers? The solid weight of his arm beneath her breasts made her conscious of their aching fullness. If it weren't for the constrictive lace she would be able to feel the soft friction of his body hair against the sensitive undercurves. All he needed to do was move his hand up slightly and the rounded flesh would be pressing into his palm...

She wriggled, trying to ease the ache her thoughts aroused. The saddle of his hips straddled her soft bottom, a tiny space preserving the modesty that the thin fabric of modern underwear would have denied them. Olivia didn't doubt that that space was deliberate on his part. She was curious but those few millimetres might as well have been a yawning chasm. If she shifted herself back into the masculine cusp of his body she would be making a choice. If he was awake and aroused, her movement would be construed as an invitation... if not, well, that would be the ultimate form of rejection. She would rather lie here in agony than accept *that* risk.

Unfortunately it *was* agony. There was no way she was going to fall asleep any time soon. Her skin felt super-sensitive, absorbing every vibration of the man behind her and translating it into a tingling heat that spread inexorably over her entire body. The air temperature was fast becoming irrelevant.

'What's the matter?' The low rumble froze her into stillness.

I'm in love with you and I desperately want you to make me feel loved, desired, fulfilled...

'Nothing.'

'*Nothing* is making you squirm about like a bug in a hot frying-pan?'

Better the frying-pan than the fire!

'I can't get comfortable.' She settled on a semi-truth. 'I'm too hot.'

There was a heartbeat's pause. When he spoke his voice was thick with velvety amusement. 'You're not hot, you're aroused. Which is not quite the same thing...'

He was laughing at her! Olivia gave a choking cry of mortification and began to struggle. The blanket was too securely tucked to give and her efforts merely tangled her limbs with his, promoting the contact she had been so rigidly trying to avoid. As Jordan's hand landed on her breast she stilled again, not daring to breathe.

'Turn over.'

'No.' It was the merest whisper, a foolish denial as his fingers drifted over the thin lace and found the satiny tip of her breast. His touch was very soft and gentle but her response was not. The rough pad of his thumb outlined the budding contour, drawing it tighter.

'But you want to...' His hand contracted with delicious skill.

'I *want* to get off this mountain,' she said shakily. 'But we can't always have what we want.'

'You can in this case. All you have to do is turn over and take it.' His hand moved, splaying out over her flat stomach, feeling the deep muscular tension there, massaging slowly until Olivia uttered a soft, ragged sound of helpless pleasure.

'Why are you doing this?' she moaned, arching involuntarily against his hand.

'Because I want what *you* want...' His fingertips trailed a fiery path up to her raised shoulder and pulled, a strong, steady motion that slowly pressed her narrow back flat on to the cotton-covered foam mattress.

'No...you can't...' Olivia was suddenly deathly afraid that this wasn't real. Jordan hovered over her, the dark, shadowy lover of her intimate dreams, his muscled chest rising from her side, a wall of steel sheathed in living silk, his blond head haloed a faint nimbus of light from the glowing stove, his eyes a silvery gleam in the dark oval of his face.

'I can't what?' He shifted his hips, moving himself deliberately against her sleek flank, caressing her with his boldness. 'Want you? Need you? Why? Is it forbidden? Is the fact that you arouse me so impossible for you to believe?'

'I... I'm not very good at this,' she stammered, panicking. The only thing worse than knowing your dream was out of reach was suddenly having it within your grasp!

His finger touched her mouth, tracing the trembling contours. 'Who told you that?'

Her past rose up to taunt her. 'I . . . I don't know what you expect me to be——' His mouth covered hers, absorbing her uncertainty. It was warm and hard, thorough and expert.

'Yourself,' he murmured, when he had briefly satisfied her hunger only to leave her longing for more. 'Just be yourself . . .'

'And what if it's not enough?' In the dark, in his arms, with the taste of him like wine on her tongue, it seemed easy to express her fears.

'It *won't* be.' He shocked her with the stark assurance. Prepared for her swift recoil, he restrained her with his big body, thrusting a heavy thigh across hers while his hand caught her flailing arm. 'I *will* want more. But you can give it to me, if you'll just give yourself a *chance* . . . if you'll just trust me . . .'

He straddled her completely, supporting his weight on his braced arms so that he didn't crush her, grinding his hips softly into hers, enticing her with his erotic actions and whispered words of reckless invitation. He ravished her body with his hot, slow kisses as he ravished her mind with his wicked encouragement.

'Come on, baby, that's right, let *go* . . .' he murmured as he felt her go under, dragged out of her depth by the swift cross-currents of desire, floundering briefly until she finally stopped fighting and began to flow with the inevitable tide. 'Touch me . . . feel me . . . let me see all that passion you keep hidden inside . . .'

He drew her hand across his chest, letting her feel the rapid thud of his heart, then he bent his head and nuzzled at the lush swell of her breasts above the transparent lace, teasing the creamy softness with his faintly abrasive jaw. 'Be whatever you want to be. Be wild, be free, be *angry*, if that's the way that wanting me makes you feel. I won't be shocked, baby. I need to know that you're opening more than just your body to me . . .'

Olivia was lost. Her hands slid to his hard waist as he moved above her, the forgotten blankets sliding down

he powerful arch of his back as he let her feel his weight,
forcing her to accept the certain knowledge that he intended to be as wild and uninhibited as he was inviting
her to be, the violent, untameable passion of his nature
devoted totally to the physical pleasure of the moment.

He said other things, graphically erotic things that
made her blush in the dark as he stripped off the only
impediments to their merging flesh, calling her 'baby'
in a thick, harsh, voice that was almost a snarl. She didn't
care if he was using the appellation because he couldn't
remember who she was—she hardly recognised herself,
and he made her feel anything *but* babyish. She had never
realised a man could be so violently aroused that he
trembled, pleaded, surrendered to a woman as if *she* were
the stronger sex. She discovered she liked him savage
and greedy and a little out of control. But even with his
surrender he dominated. Even out of control he controlled, balancing his fierce sexual aggression with his
innate sensitivity. He was rough, but he was sure, never
hurting her in spite of the disparity in their sizes. He
shaped and formed her as if she were a living sculpture,
rewarding her with melting ecstasy as she rippled beneath his talented hands.

Only once did the dream falter, when Jordan reared
back, kneeling between her parted thighs, holding her
flat on the narrow bunk with a broad hand spread across
her shimmering breasts when she tried to bring him back
to her.

Olivia drew a sobbing breath and, feeling utterly exposed in the darkness, tried to cover herself. With catlike
skill he homed in on the vague movements, clasping her
wrists in his free hand, bending to brush his mouth
against the soft curls she had attempted to protect. She
jerked at the intimacy and he did it again, lingering ex-
quisitely until she quivered and her wrists went lax in his
firm grasp.

'Red as fire,' he guessed huskily, tasting the spicy tang
of her submission, 'and just as hot. You're a woman of

the elements, Livvy—earth, wind and fire...cool as wate
only when you remember to be...' He knelt back again
resisting the yearning of her hips.

'Why are you doing this?' she panted.

'Making love to you?'

'No—*stopping*!' she burst out, too wild with frus
tration to fear his reply.

He lifted her captive wrists and leaned forward to kis
them. '*Noblesse oblige*...'

'Oh, God, you said you weren't going to b
noble——'

Her ragged disgust almost made him laugh wit
exultant triumph.

'Not in the sense you mean. You've offered me th
privilege of your body; the least I can do is exercise m
responsibility——'

'I won't let you do this——' Olivia wrenched her hand
free with a violence that took him by surprise, as di
the tug that tumbled him back down to her.

'Do what?' He let her wrap her arms around him
enjoying the softness of her breasts and the contrast o
their little hard dagger-points digging into his chest. He
thighs welcomed his heavy arousal, parting only jus
enough to trap him in a silky prison of exquisite friction

'Stop.'

'You're going to *order* me to make love to you
Command me to climax?'

He *was* laughing! She could feel his chest vibrating
She would soon wipe that smile off his face. Now sh
knew the extent of her power she was wild to use it. Sh
rubbed her face against his taunting chest and bit int
the smooth muscle, using her teeth the way he had use
his to torment her swollen breasts before he had sweetl
suckled away the ache. She shifted her thighs, letting th
male weight of him slide against her fiery heart. H
groaned, exciting her, seducing himself.

A few more intense moments and he put a stop to th
delicious torture that was getting totally out of hand

wrapping his hand into her tangled curls and wrenching her head away from his throbbing body.

'Olivia, perhaps I'd better make it clear exactly what specific responsibility I had in mind... Unless you also intend to command me to make you most thoroughly pregnant, I suggest you let me attend to it... *now*!'

He kissed her astonished open mouth once more, hard, before he got off the bed and walked, with a rigidly awkward gait, over to his pack. After he had raided his survival kit he paused to open the fire-door, letting a rich, warm yellow shaft lighten the gloom.

'I want to see you,' he said huskily as he turned back. 'I want to see this wild mountain-woman who ensnares unwary travellers in her toils and forces them to become her love-slaves.'

Olivia blushed, as much at his words as at the sight of him, unashamedly aroused and gloriously male, blatantly enjoying her sultry-eyed study of his anatomy as he strolled lazily back to her. She tore her gaze away to the hand that brushed his hard flank.

'You do believe in being prepared, don't you?' She knew she should be applauding his forethought but somehow she also felt offended at the evidence of his lack of spontaneity. She stiffened as he kneeled beside her again, obviously intent on taking up where they had left off, placing the small package by the pillow.

'With you, I had to be,' he growled tenderly, soothing her doubts. 'I didn't know where or when, but I knew that we would be lovers some time soon, and that our coming together would be so intensely pleasurable for both of us that nothing on earth would stop the consummation, ready or not...'

He watched the familiar warming of her creamy skin with a flare of satisfaction. He wondered whether she would still blush for him when they were totally familiar with each other's bodies and emotions. He hoped so. He liked the blatant acknowledgement of her physical awareness of him.

He bent and kissed her soft warm mouth, luxuriatin
in her swift response, easing them gradually, beautifull·
back into the serious rhythms of lovemaking, exhibitin
a frank pleasure that made Olivia feel utterly liberatec
How could she have ever believed that he didn't wai
her? It was there, in every kiss, every caress, every quiv·
that shuddered through his powerful frame as he too
her again and again to the very edge of bliss before witl
drawing and beginning all over again until she wild.
seized the initiative and forced him to concede victor
to them both. He had made her weep but she had mac
him moan—thick, discordant sounds that were like a
excruciatingly sweet accompaniment to music in her sou

Olivia was stunned by the force of her abandon. Loga
had never even touched such depths in her—or perhaj
they hadn't even existed then—and her disillusionmer
with him had made her wary of all males for a lon
time. She had not found it difficult to curb her largel
unawakened sexual impulses. Celibacy had been an eas
option, even when Gabriel had come along. Her lov
for him had proved another illusion, a mental infatt
ation that had only confirmed her view of herself as
woman with a low sex-drive and high emotion:
vulnerability.

In the brief span of a night Jordan showed her a star·
lingly different image of herself: sensual and sensuou·
demanding, as capable of delivering pleasure as of joy
fully receiving it. It didn't seem to matter that no wor
of love was spoken. The things that Olivia didn't dar
say were too perfectly expressed in other ways, her sens·
revelling in the discovery of this new and intensely ai
ticulate language of love. Jordan once again proved hi
artistic ability, creating the carnal pleasures for her i
bold chiaroscuro, the light of ecstasy pure and white
the dark shadings of passion a thick, hot velvet tha
smothered her senses with extravagant delight.

The sleep he had claimed they needed was a long tim
in coming, but then, as far as Olivia was concerned, sh

didn't care if they *never* got off this mountain. Curled back against Jordan's heart, she felt deeply content, a world of difference between this tenderly assured embrace and the one that had caused her so much agony earlier. As she sank into sleep she allowed herself the forbidden luxury of believing that this was only the beginning, that Jordan, too, had given something irredeemable of himself this night...

It was the sound that woke her, the rhythmic thump-thump that suddenly seemed to explode into her vivid fantasies. Olivia sat bolt upright, almost crowning herself on the upper bunk. Jordan was nowhere to be seen and she was immediately stricken by the fear that the whole eventful night had been merely a spiteful dream.

Then the cabin door opened and he was there, bringing with him a miniature gale that slammed the door behind her.

'Helicopter coming in,' he said succinctly, when he saw her heavy-eyed look. 'It looks as though we're getting a quick ride down.'

It was on the tip of Olivia's tongue to say that she'd rather go the slow way, but then it occurred to her that Jordan seemed vaguely uneasy... regretful? A *frisson* of tension shivered through her pleasantly aching muscles.

'Here. Your clothes are dry. I'll just make sure this fire is completely out...'

Was it thoughtfulness or awkwardness that led him to turn his back while she pulled on her crumpled trousers and sweater? He certainly wasn't the extravagantly praiseful lover of a few hours before. Not even a good-morning smile, let alone a kiss! Olivia's apprehension deepened. A brief look out the window showed her that the sun was well up, but weakened considerably by the filter of low cloud that hovered a few hundred metres above the hut. How long had Jordan been up and about? Why hadn't he woken her softly, as he had lulled her to sleep? Why the hint of grim purposefulness in his move-

ments, as if he couldn't wait to get away from the scen
of their brief idyll?

At the door she took one last look around. The hu
looked exactly as it had when they had arrived—stark
untouched by the small human drama acted out withi
its walls. It seemed like an inanimate reflection c
Jordan's stern constraint. Unversed in the rules c
morning-after behaviour, Olivia wasn't sure how to reac
but she knew she had to say *something* ...

'Jordan——'

'Later, Olivia. We can straighten this out later, w.
we have the time. Right now we have to get going. Duc
and run.'

He accompanied his instructions with a firm pus
which Olivia didn't resist. 'Straighten this out'? He mad
the whole thing sound like a polite misunderstanding.

Olivia's heart was in her mouth as she scurried ove
to the helicopter, noting the Pendragon crest on the doo
as the pilot leaned over to push it open. She swung :
wider and turned as Jordan joined her, his height almos
bent double against the chilling up-draught. She smile
at him tentatively and was faintly shocked when he re
sponded with a slow, serious curve of his mouth tha
didn't lighten his sombre tawny gaze. He briefly cuppe
her jaw, taking her by surprise with the roughness of hi
touch, before letting her go and gesturing impatientl
towards the cockpit.

The pilot had radioed ahead and as they landed o
the lawn of the big house they were met by William an
Beverly, and their cluster of curious guests. To Olivia'
discomfort William's welcome was rife with his par
ticular brand of innuendo and this time she had n
righteous innocence to protect her. She was sure her sin
were written large across her flushed face and Jorda
didn't help with his terse uncommunicativeness.

To her further dismay William then rushed Jordan of
to some vital meeting in Taupo that he urgently had ha
to reschedule—something to do with Pendragon Famil

Trust business—leaving Olivia suspended in the midst of her emotional limbo.

The only thing left to do, she decided as she showered and changed and picked uninterestedly at brunch before going down to the studio as if it were just another perfectly ordinary day, was hope. At least hope was a strong and positive emotion. No more letting her fears devour her courage.

But she had reckoned without Beverly.

'Abandon hope all ye who enter' might as well have been mounted above the studio door when Olivia walked in and found the other woman standing in front of the impotent *Jester*, studying it with a blood-curdling interest.

She turned as Olivia entered and said, in a pleasant voice that reeked of deadly sympathy, 'You really haven't caught him at all, have you? I suppose you're thankful for that now. You must do another—a proper one this time—if only you can get Jordan to agree; you know how terribly awkward he is about publicity—but perhaps, for *you*, he just might change his mind...'

CHAPTER TEN

'PERSONAL triumph...'

Olivia savoured the art-gallery owner's flattering words. After what happened here last time she didn't think that Sam Findlay would ever allow her to set foot, much less painting, over his precious threshold again. True, it wasn't a solo exhibition and she had only been a last-minute substitute when another artist had withdrawn, but still it was a confirmation that her tantrum had caused more torment to herself than anyone else. In fact, Sam Findlay had been surprisingly gracious when Olivia had fronted up with an apology on her lips and half a dozen paintings tucked under her arm.

Of course, it was *The Jester* that had proved the real passport back into his favour. One look at it and he had signed her up on the spot, even though she hadn't intended to plunge back into the public arena just yet. Now the painting that she once had consigned to mental oblivion occupied pride of place among the Taupo abstracts and the scenic watercolours that she had worked up from the sketches she had made during her time with Jordan...

Jordan...

It always came back to Jordan. She couldn't bring herself to forgive him but neither could she forget him. During the whole three weeks she had been back in Auckland she had daily expected a raging hulk to turn up on her doorstep, demanding the confrontation she had been too cowardly to face, the apology he so richly deserved. But perhaps he, like Olivia, was so sickened by her actions that he couldn't bear the pain of personal confrontation. Perhaps she would receive a cold letter

170

from some classy Pendragon lawyer threatening to sue... perhaps she should write to *him* ...

Oh, *God*, how she had wanted him to come!

What he had done was terrible, but what she had done had been even worse. Only another artist could appreciate the true nature of her appalling act. She had attacked the one part of him that was utterly innocent and had destroyed something potentially beautiful in the process, something that no amount of physical reparation could ever restore.

It was no excuse that she had been in the grip of a devastating pain herself. Her actions had not only been pointless but actually criminal, emotional as well as physical vandalism. The fiery rage that blinded her then had long since died into cold ashes. Even Beverly, hoping for the worst, couldn't have expected such an explosion from the last weapon in her depleted arsenal, the casual revelation that Jordan was the 'the Jester', the art critic who had publicly annihilated Olivia's reputation.

At first Olivia had resolutely refused to believe the other woman's calculated spite. That Beverly was prepared to go so far in her fanatical desire to destroy all possible links between Olivia and Jordan was all the more reason that everything she said be regarded with deep suspicion. She had said that she was the only one, bar the newspaper editor, who knew his true identity. Why would Jordan confide in a woman he regarded with cynical distrust?

But the pity with which Beverly had regarded Olivia's disbelief had been chillingly genuine—the first evidence of real emotion that she had shown—a kind of empathetic feminine acceptance of the inevitability of male betrayal. Perhaps she had found out the truth, or what she thought was the truth, by accident. Surely she wouldn't utter such an outrageous lie if she knew that it could easily be disproved?

After letting Beverly's words nibble away at her shaky confidence, Olivia had borrowed one of the staff cars

and driven over to Jordan's studio. She had needed to
touch and admire his work again, to surround herself
with the awe-inspiring evidence of his artistic integrity,
the warmth of his spirit.

She had touched it all right! Olivia nervously smoothed
down her skirt with suddenly damp hands as she remembered what form her admiration had taken! Roz
had helped her choose this dress for the opening of the
exhibition and she wasn't quite sure it suited her. It was
black, flimsy and flirty, the half-circle mini-skirt the
briefest she had sported in years. Roz, in contrast, had
worn subdued green velvet, demure of neck and hem, a
switch of red hair cunningly woven into her own and
plaited meekly on top of her head.

'Now, Olivia, what are you doing here on your own?
You're not doing your job. Circulate! Circulate! A lot
of people are asking to meet you!' Sam Findlay thrust
a brimming glass of champagne into her hand. 'You
know, it was very, very naughty of you to insist on that
price for *The Jester*; I told you you were undervaluing
it. I could have sold it ten times over for twice the price.'

Olivia didn't feel like telling him that it was a necessary
part of her personal therapy. Selling it cheaply was a
form of masochistic revenge. She needed something to
bolster her pride after the way she had destroyed any
hope of obtaining the commission she had risked so
much for.

When she had arrived back from Jordan's studio,
angry, hurt, ashamed, with scraped hands and hair
powered with the evidence of her rage, she had demanded to see Alun Pendragon and lied brazenly about
a family emergency without the slightest twinge of guilt.
When she had told him that his portrait was finished
and there was no reason for her to come back, however,
he had been outraged.

'Finished? *Finished*?' He jabbed a finger in the air in
the direction of the easel that stood in the corner of the
room. 'It isn't halfway done, even I can see that!'

'*That* isn't my painting——'

'I'm not senile yet, young lady!' He was well into his stride. 'I know you've been floundering ar—hey! Where do you think you're going?'

He soon found out. Alun Pendragon's jaw dropped when she stormed back in with her alternative canvas.

'*This* is *my* painting. *That* one was for *you*.'

He had howled. It wasn't as bizarre as *The Jester* but it was still distinctly off-beat. He wasn't sitting in the sombre, hackneyed pose of dignity but was instead captured in the act of laying down the law in his own inimitable style. The familiar jabbing finger pointed straight out of the canvas, the eyes narrowed to an accusing glitter, the elegant clothes bunched at the aggressively hunched shoulders, his features and body elongated to exaggerate the energy and intensity of his will-power. He leaned, looking as though, any minute, he was going to lunge forward out of the canvas and take the viewer by the throat. All Olivia's exasperation, but also her grudging admiration, had gone into the painting.

'I look like a damned hooligan!' The elder Pendragon's ire had finally died down to a grumbling petulance.

'Yes, you do rather, don't you?' Olivia's patience had long been exhausted. All she wanted to do was get out of there before she burst into tears.

'Hmmm.' He gave her another one of his shrewd up-and-under looks, a nameless emotion glinting in the ageless eyes. 'At least I don't look like a dried-up old has-been, I suppose.' He pursed his lips at her blind lack of response. 'Does Jordan like it?'

Why did he assume that she had shown Jordan? She had reared up on her pride and pain. 'I don't give a damn what that wretched, lying, contemptible coward of a son of yours thinks...about anything! He can go to the devil—you both can! Why don't you two solve your own problems before you start creating them for other people?'

She had left him spluttering and no doubt mortally offended but at least she had vented her spleen.

'Olivia, are you listening to me?'

'Pardon?' From the offended expression on his face Sam considered what he had been saying to be something of vital importance.

'I *said* that, going on tonight's sales, we don't even have to worry about the reviews. "Jester" can't dip his pen in vitriol this time without it coming across like sour grapes . . .'

Olivia's mouth had gone so dry that she had difficulty swallowing her champagne. She had refused to even entertain the cringing thought that Jordan might come. God, what a scene he could make if he chose! She quickly gulped the rest of her champagne and grabbed another glass from a passing tray.

Of course he wouldn't turn up, she told herself stoutly, not unless he planned on totally blowing his cover. He might have an almighty weapon to brandish over her head, but she had powerful protection. For a moment she had forgotten the vitriolic little note she had rapped out on his typewriter, tucked away in the one corner of his studio he hadn't shown her. She had left his damning files exposed, her hunt-and-peck method of typing restricting her message to one of barren hatred: 'Now we're even, Jester!'

They weren't. In spite of what he had done her love was proving to be as much a survivor of disaster as her talent. But Olivia couldn't keep on looking back over her shoulder, mourning all the 'ifs'. She had been more prolific during the past three weeks than she had ever been, still working recklessly alla prima, sometimes being delighted and at other times disheartened by the results, but always *working* . . .

Giving in to Sam's urging, Olivia dutifully began circulating again, cheating a little by spending most of the time chatting to various members of her family.

So secure was she in their warmth that she was taken completely off guard when a cultured voice interrupted them.

'Olivia, can I have a word?'

'William!' After a moment of shock Olivia quickly edged him away from her insatiably curious relatives. 'What are you doing here?' She looked frantically around. 'Are you alone?'

William pulled a rueful face. 'Beverly and I aren't engaged any more.'

'Oh—er—I'm——' The word sorry was swamped by a hot rise of bitter satisfaction in Olivia's throat.

'Delighted? Ecstatic?' William smiled at her struggle to be polite.

'Well...' Olivia managed a lame smile in return. 'Did you break it off or...?'

'Or did she dump me? Actually, I'm not sure, it was sort of half and half, and way past due. There was this almighty row just after you left...'

'Oh?' Olivia's eyes took on a glazed look.

'Mmm. I've never *seen* Alun so furious at Beverly——'

'*Alun* was?'

'It was that terrific portrait you did. Beverly made some cuttingly derogatory comments about it and Alun took exception. That led to a bit of mud-slinging and everything sort of degenerated into some unfortunate truth-telling. When I didn't back her up Beverly told me I was a spineless jerk and I told her she was a greedy parasite...and that was that.' He dismissed his former fiancée with a callous ease that put Beverly firmly in her place—nowhere, thought Olivia with vengeful satisfaction. 'Maybe she decided that she'd outlived her influence when Jordan said he'd decided to take on the Pendragon Art Commission——'

'*What*? But ... but why?'

'Why don't you ask me?'

The damp champagne glass slipped through her fingers and shattered on the parquet floor as the question caressed the nape of her neck. Fortunately the volume level in the large gallery was so high that only those in the immediate vicinity turned to see what the noise was. William met her accusing eyes with a grin and a shrug as he melted away into the crowd.

'Well? Aren't you going to ask?'

Olivia began to walk away without looking behind her. She was stopped by a thick arm coiling around her waist, drawing her back against a familiar, hard length.

'Ask me,' he persisted.

She discovered she was shaking, and she didn't know whether it was rage or fear.

'Let me go.'

'Never.'

'Let me go or I'll scream.' She meant it, too, the pressure swiftly building inside her.

'Scream away. We've made a scene before in this gallery, remember? It'll probably be good for business, although you seem to be doing pretty well without the gimmicks.'

Trust him, on this day of triumph, to remind her of past defeats. She imagined the anger and contempt in his eyes and began to struggle.

'You b——' Another hand wrapped around her mouth. They were attracting a little more attention now, the seething redhead being tenderly manhandled by the big blond brute. Olivia could have cried with relief when her brother Hugh suddenly appeared in front of them, braced for protective action.

'Is this what they call "performance art"?' As always Hugh's steely intent was masked in a soft, deceptively gentle voice. 'I didn't know you went in for that sort of thing, Pendragon.'

Olivia shouldn't have been surprised that they knew each other; after all, as a commercial lawyer Hugh moved in the same corporate circles as Jordan used to.

The man behind her was perceptive; his tone was conciliatory, but equally quiet and purposeful. 'I don't. I sculpt...under the name of Junius. I also used to review galleries, in the guise of 'the Jester'. And I'm your sister's lover. I need to talk to her, but she doesn't want to listen. I think, for the sake of both our happiness, she should.'

There was no sign of Hugh relaxing but his frost-grey eyes narrowed. 'Let her go and perhaps we can negotiate an acceptable compromise.'

It was Hugh as his most lawyerish. *Negotiation*? Olivia shuddered. In three short phrases Jordan had effectively disposed of any threat she could pose him. He had deliberately wrecked his own anonymity in order to gain the upper hand.

'I don't want a compromise. If I can't have all...I'd rather have nothing.'

'I'm sure there's somewhere more private where we can discuss this like reasonable adults,' Hugh, the traitor, was saying. 'Sam has his office on the mezzanine floor; perhaps there...'

The moment the two men moved Olivia grabbed her chance. A quick wriggle, a frantic crawl through a thicket of immaculately shod feet and a mad dash and she was dragging her twin towards the door.

'We have to get out of here!'

'But we can't...you said Sam was going to make a speech.' Roz dug her heels into the Persian runner in the narrow foyer. 'You can't run out in the middle of things. What happened?'

'Not what. *Who*!' In a few succinct phrases Olivia explained the horror. To her dismay, for she hadn't made the mistake of bottling up her feelings a second time, Roz proved strangely reluctant to co-operate. 'Don't you think you maybe—er—owe it to him to hear what he——?'

'No' Olivia was on the verge of hysteria. 'For God's sake, Roz, are you going to lend me your car or not?'

To her relief Roz abruptly caved in at the sight of a few desperate tears, but no way was she going to let Olivia get behind a wheel.

By the time Roz had driven her frantic sister back to her studio she was infected with the same brand of hysterical paranoia. Drastic measures were called for, she decided as she bundled Olivia inside.

The Jordan Pendragon who thundered on the door twenty minutes later was a great deal different from the vigorous, sexy individualist who had inhabited his Taupo residence. To the woman who nervously opened the door he was intimidatingly elegant and formal. He was dressed in a dark blue suit that was unmistakably Italian to the tutored eye, and silk to boot. His shirt was primly white, his tie, also silk, striped grey and blue. He looked like a million dollars, which was probably less than his worth, cool and controlled—if you didn't look at his face. That was strained and weary, in a grim, stoic kind of way that said things were going to get a hell of a lot tougher before they got better.

He didn't let her speak. His curious tawny blue eyes wandered over the flirty black dress and tousled curls and his mouth compressed impatiently.

'Are you going to let me in? I *could* strip that sexy piece of nothing off you and make love to you right here on the doorstep until you beg for mercy...'

Eyebrows arched haughtily. 'Or I could call the police. That would be another option.'

His eyes crawled over her face. It was as pale as cream. 'It would, but unless they lock me up for the next forty years it's not going to solve your problem.'

'What do you want?' she said abruptly, unnerved by that stare.

'Don't you know?'

'I——'

He cursed, repressing a brief surge of violence. 'I made some mistakes, I want to right them.' His voice roughened. 'I'm in love. I need to know if there's a chance my feeling is returned. I am bleeding to death, dammit, and I'm asking for a chance for a transfusion...'

There was a fierce glitter in his eyes and a shake in his voice that he made no attempt to hide. God, was he going to *cry* ...?

'Jordan——'

'So are you going to let me see her now, Roz? Or do you want to put me all the way through your meat-grinder first? I don't care, as long as I get to see her...'

Roz slumped. 'You know?'

'Of course I *know*,' he snarled at her. 'I'm in love with *her*. Not *you*. I couldn't give a damn about *you*...' He gave a rough grunt, closing his eyes, as he realised where his temper had led him. Oh, to hell with being reasonable!

He pushed past her easily and looked around. Roz touched his arm and tilted her head in the direction of the screen that blocked off the bed from the rest of the room. He took her into a bear-hug and kissed her un-blushing cheek just as Olivia peeked irresistibly through the crack in the partition. She jumped back, knocking it with her elbow, and it fell down with a resounding bang.

'Livvy, he knew it was me——' Roz hastened to re-assure her twin's expression of agonised betrayal.

'Get out, Roz.'

'What?' She frowned at him, loath to miss what she deemed was going to be a spectacular last act to a pro-duction she had had no small part in creating.

'*Out*!' Jordan gave her a shove, not taking his eyes off Olivia. 'We don't need you. We never did.'

What was he, a mind-reader?

'Sorry, Liv.' Roz cast her twin a sympathetic look that was totally wasted.

'I suppose you've come about your sculpture,' Olivia wavered, when it seemed that Jordan was waiting fo something.

'It wasn't a sculpture. It was only a piece of stone.'

Only stone? The ground cut beneath her feet by hi casual dismissal of his first passion, Olivia floundered 'I...I broke it.'

She remembered the weighty feel of the sledge hammer, the fury that had pulsed through her as she had attacked the symbol of her seduction—the stone from which he was drawing the entwined couple he had talked about.

'You underestimate your effort—on people as well a things,' he said drily. 'You reduced it to a pile of fine rubble.'

Olivia flushed painfully. Roz's demure green velve dress suddenly felt awfully hot. 'I'm sorry. I found you reviews. I...I went a little crazy for a while.'

'Only for a while? You've driven me *permanently* crazy.' He was still talking across the width of the room standing very still, using only his voice to communicate Where she had expected anger there was merely sadness contempt—compassion.

'You lied to me...' Her voice was stifled with confusion. Somehow she couldn't find the rage of indignation that had sustained her thus far. *He had come.* Though she had run from it, this was what she had been waiting for, longing for...

This time he didn't argue semantics. 'You have every right to be angry with me, Olivia. But please don't shut me out. At least hear me out. If you still want to send me away afterwards, I'll go, no fuss, I promise...' His mouth twisted. 'Although I suppose you have no reason to believe anything I say...'

'She said——' Olivia took a trembling breath. She didn't have to say who 'she' was. 'She said that you felt your review was directly responsible for my collapse— that you felt so guilty——'

'I got drunk.'

'I beg your pardon?'

Jordan turned abruptly half away from her, stopping as he spotted the sculpture that Roz had bought her, pausing to touch it with a briefly ironic smile. 'The night I wrote that review. I'd been to see your exhibition and hated it—yes, I did. I could see what you were groping for but it wasn't you. I thought you were a potential great talent and I hated what you had done with it. I'd wanted to meet you for ages, but that day I just couldn't face you. If I had I might have realised what a knife-edge you were on.'

He was stroking his sculpture as if he could draw the strength to continue from it and it seemed to calm him down. His voice became sardonic.

'So I did the time-honoured thing. I got blind, black, roaring drunk. Then I stumbled back to the editorial offices and poured all the bile into a typewriter. I was going to re-write it in the morning when I was thinking and seeing straight again. Oh, it still would have been very negative but it wouldn't have been so... *bitter*. Unfortunately I passed out at my hotel and overslept and someone else "helpfully" filed the copy for me. By the time I'd got into the office it was too late. I could have published a partial retraction but I thought that it would only generate *more* negative publicity...'

Olivia had drifted closer, magnetised by this almost ceremonial baring of his soul.

'I wasn't there at the gallery that day by accident,' he admitted rawly. 'I was there to see you. I wanted to explain. Then I couldn't... you were so vulnerable and helpless... So I just tried to keep you safe and prayed that some time in the future I'd be able to set the record straight. Only the time never seemed to be right. When I saw that painting you—Roz—brought down to Taupo, I literally quailed. I was delighted for you and devastated for myself. However you felt about me as a man you would always hate the memory of what I'd done.

'The whole time you were there my identity hung ove
our heads like a Sword of Damocles. I knew I was takin
advantage of your ignorance but I thought if I coul
make you fall in love with me before you found out tha
would cushion the blow for both of us. But after tha
night on Tongariro I realised I'd been kidding myse
that what you didn't know couldn't hurt you. It wa
hurting me. You were taking all the risks while I wa
busily protecting myself. I suppose I felt . . .' he shrugge
awkwardly as he expressed the alien concept '. . . ur
worthy. Even then I grabbed the first opportunity t
put off the inevitable. In a way, Beverly did me
favour——'

'A *favour*?' Olivia's mouth twisted as she remem
bered the nightmare she had endured.

He regarded her warily. 'We had a nasty little con
frontation before Will and I left for Taupo that day w
came down off the mountain. I made the mistake c
telling her that I loved you and that if she didn't cur
her behaviour then I'd ensure that *she* was the one t
be banished from the Pendragon enclave. I didn't kno
then that she'd snooped and found out about my bein
"Jester"——'

Olivia was staring at him, her eyes wide and dark a
jade. He loved her? *He loved her*! He could toss it s
casually into the conversation, as if she had alway
known it, always accepted it as a proven fact.

He loved her?

'My father asked me to buy it for him, you know. *Th
Jester*,' he added when he saw her shocked confusio
'He thinks it's a great joke.' His smile was gently sel
mocking. 'It's odd, but, for all his bitter opposition t
the way I run my life, I think he's actually quite prou
of me, although I don't suppose I'll ever hear him adm
it out loud. I told him I thought you'd captured hir
perfectly in the portrait, no one could look at it withou
knowing that he was a man who had created his ow
destiny . . . if not his dynasty. He actually laughed, an

hen he had the gall to mutter something about needing
statue to complement it. I have a nasty feeling he's
oing to make a thorough nuisance of himself until he's
nmortalised in stone somewhere appropriately
rominent—perhaps across from the Beehive in
Vellington so the Parliamentarians can look out on a
onstant reproach if the Honours List doesn't come up
o scratch.'

His teasing smile sobered. 'I realised that you were
ight, I hadn't been looking at his art sponsorship scheme
s an opportunity but as the thin end of an unwelcome
vedge. Maybe Beverly's presence, too, had the effect of
lurring my vision. I realised that I could do great things
vith it, use it to expand my life rather than diminish
t... perhaps even educate my Philistine father to ap-
reciate art for its own sake in the process! If I do it, I
vant to do it well. Loving you has taught me that I can't
ive with half-measures...'

He loved her?

Olivia was dizzy, elated and appalled by the responsi-
ility. That meant that she could hurt him, too, by her
ctions and emotions, probably had...

'You—I put *The Jester* in the exhibition because I... I
vanted to show you I didn't care——' she admitted
lowly.

'But instead it showed to me that you *did*,' he inter-
upted firmly. 'At least you felt *something* for me,
omething strong enough to make you openly flaunt a
ery private revenge. I hate the circumstances that made
ne the inspiration, but I'm proud to be associated with
uch a superb piece of work, proud enough to admit it
o the whole damned world if necessary!'

'Does that mean that "Jester" is going to give me a
;ood review tomorrow?' Olivia said staunchly, before
he wild, intoxicating happiness overflowed into loving
orgiveness.

She shouldn't make it too easy for him. It might be
:ruel but she needed to be very sure what she was taking

on. She would need to be strong to love a man li[ke]
Jordan, fiercely independent and intensely passiona[te]
and she would need to be very secure in that strength[.]

'I don't know. I don't know who's writing the revie[w]
these days——'

'You mean it's not you?'

'Not any more,' he said quietly. 'After what ha[p]
pened with you I lost my taste for reviewing, or perha[ps]
it was my nerve. I certainly lost my detachment and tha[t's]
vital for a reviewer. Unfortunately the paper owns t[he]
copyright on the name and just gets someone else to wr[ite]
the columns.'

'But you were a good reviewer.' When had she mov[ed]
close enough to touch him? To be close and not to tou[ch]
was impossible, although she found his immaculate a[p]
pearance somewhat daunting. He solved the problem [by]
picking up her hovering hands and sliding them benea[th]
his unbuttoned jacket.

'I was arrogant, careless, I abused a trust——'

'Not mine. You were honest. You *were*,' she insist[ed]
when he shook his head, the muscles of his che[st]
bunching under her fingertips. 'Why do you think it hu[rt]
so much? It was ugly, but it was the truth. I was da[b]
bling, fooling around with something I really did[n't]
understand or even really care to. I was afraid and i[n]
stead of facing my fears I tried to pretend they did[n't]
exist. I was wrong and I wouldn't admit it. I was si[ck]
and I wouldn't admit it. God knows how long I wou[ld]
have gone on if you hadn't held up that mirror to m[y]
futility——'

'Oh, God, Olivia——' His arms went around her a[nd]
held her, hard, his face burrowing into her fiery curl[s.]
'You kill me with your honesty. I don't bloody well d[e]
serve you.'

'No, you don't.' Her words were muffled in his che[st]
as she inhaled his familiar male fragrance, mixed wi[th]
the musky odour of perspiration. He had be[en]

wretchedly nervous, she realised, sweating buckets for all the brave face he had put on at the gallery.

'But you'll take me just the same...'

'Take you where?'

'Here, there, anywhere...' At his rusty chuckle she tilted her head back. His eyes were almost pure gold, edged with a narrow band of blue. 'You realise what I'm asking you, Olivia?'

'To live with you and be your love?' she said whimsically.

He shuddered on a laugh. 'I wouldn't dare. Your brother has already outlined the legal requirements of loving you.'

'You don't have to take any notice of Hugh.' Olivia's heart was willing to make the sacrifice. She loved Jordan as he was, not as her fond fantasies would have him.

'The hell I don't—he's almost as big as I am!' Jordan gave her an admonitory shake, his grin sobering as he watched the thoughts flit across her expressive face. 'Do you imagine that I'd take any risk, however small, of letting you slip through my fingers again? I told you I wasn't noble. I don't want castles in the air, I want good, solid foundations on which to build a life together. That means rings and vows and family approval and maybe children to build our own little offshoot of the Pendragon dynasty...'

Somehow Olivia couldn't quite picture herself as the matriarch of any kind of dynasty—or one of the powerful Pendragons, come to that. She had no trouble, however, dreamily picturing herself at Jordan's side, raising a golden-haired brood as vigorous and vital as their father, and painting up a joyous storm...

'Is there space for me in your studio?'

'There is now I've cleared out the rubble,' he reminded her wickedly and laughed when she flushed uncomfortably. 'I'd only just started on the sculpture, Olivia, a few chisel-marks was all it was. I'll admit I was furious enough to want to smash a few things myself at the time, but that was because I thought I'd lost you, not because you'd destroyed a hunk of stone. But, if you still feel you owe me, I won't stand in your way. In fact, you can stand in mine . . . you can pose for it . . .'

'You told me you didn't need me,' Olivia murmured as he tilted her off balance and walked her backwards, with lascivious intent, over the flattened screen.

'I need you all the time . . .' It was the simple truth, the hunger in his eyes igniting her own.

Olivia felt the long zip parting down her spine and the dress begin to slide very undemurely off her shoulders as the bed hit the back of her knees.

'Aren't I lucky to be getting a husband who's so clever with his hands . . . ?' she murmured, pushing at his jacket.

'We're well matched,' he said, dropping her flat on her back and peeling off the dress, studying her with a deep, thrilling satisfaction as she lay waiting for him to join her, 'in all things, in all ways. You know, the last time I shared this bed with you I ached for days afterwards.' The tawny hunger flamed a little hotter. 'This time I'm afraid you're the one who's going to ache because I don't feel capable of gentlemanly restraint . . .'

'I never mistook you for a gentleman, even dressed in your corporation suit,' teased Olivia, watching through lowered lids as he took it off with more haste than grace, throwing the expensive silk carelessly on the floor. 'Were you hoping to impress me with your sartorial elegance? You were more likely to frighten me away . . .'

He looked shaken at the prospect. 'I dressed like this because I wanted you to take me seriously,' he delighted her by saying with the utmost sincerity. He actually thought he had to dress up to impress her! 'I was going to make a deal with you. It's still yours, if you want it. If you want the Pendragon commission, Olivia, I can give it to you. William will push it through . . . my father, too, for that matter—he's convinced that you have a mellowing effect on my bull-headedness . . .'

He wistfully traced a finger along the pale lavender lace curving over her breasts. He looked up and saw her watching him and flushed, snatching his finger back and looking oddly guilty as he lay propped beside her.

'I mean it, Olivia. I can do it.'

He was touchingly earnest and with the insight that loving him had given her Olivia realised that he expected to have his generous offer flung back in his teeth. She also realised that he really did want her to do it. He believed in her. He wanted to share his love and pride in her with the whole world. She didn't need his help now, but he needed her to accept it.

'Good.'

'Good?' His gaze jerked up, startled.

'I'll take it!'

'You will?' His pleasure was cautious.

'I will.' It was a vow as binding as their marriage would be. She knew now that she was equal to any challenge he cared enough to throw at her, including that of dealing with his powerful, manipulative family. Even if Alun Pendragon had deigned to give them his blessing, he could not change his basically dominating nature, he would still do his best to shape their lives to his wishes and demands. There would be battles ahead. By giving her the Pendragon commission he would be publicly acknowledging her as an artist and, by implication, as Jordan's wife. She would use that status to protect herself and her love. She linked her arms around Jordan's strong neck. 'But only if I get some *very* urgent inspiration...'

Jordan, as usual, needed no words to provide it...

HARLEQUIN®

PRESENTS® plus

Meet Sybilla Gardner. She lives in a picturesque English village that's suddenly become too small. Gareth Seymour's returned, sending her emotions reeling back in time. She can try to avoid him, but can she resist him?

And then there's Hilary Fairfax. She's living in an isolated mountain house with Marlene, her pregnant and recently widowed cousin, *and* Conner St. George—Marlene's unwelcoming, disapproving and disturbingly attractive brother-in-law....

Sybilla and Hilary are just two of the passionate women you'll discover each month in Harlequin Presents Plus. And if you think they're passionate, wait until you meet their men!

Watch for
STRANGER FROM THE PAST by Penny Jordan
Harlequin Presents Plus # 1599

and

WHEN DRAGONS DREAM by Kathleen O'Brien
Harlequin Presents Plus # 1600

Harlequin Presents Plus
The best has just gotten better!

Available in November wherever Harlequin books are sold.

1993 Keepsake

CHRISTMAS

Stories

Capture the spirit and romance of Christmas with KEEPSAKE CHRISTMAS STORIES, a collection of three stories by favorite historical authors. The perfect Christmas gift!

Don't miss these heartwarming stories, available in November wherever Harlequin books are sold:

ONCE UPON A CHRISTMAS by Curtiss Ann Matlock
A FAIRYTALE SEASON by Marianne Willman
TIDINGS OF JOY by Victoria Pade

ADD A TOUCH OF ROMANCE TO YOUR HOLIDAY SEASON WITH KEEPSAKE CHRISTMAS STORIES!

HX93

WORDFIND #10

```
P E N D R A G O N E T Y U I
  E U P O I M N V C F G W D W
  R E R E R T Y H A I V I L O
  O S D S G H X V B E N N T L
  M Z X A U W E E R T Y T J R
  A D F W E E E R V B M E W A
  N E W Z E A L A N D B B R M
  C S D E R T G H U J T Y U I
  E S D W E R T U D O A S E W
  Z X S E X Y B N M R K L I N
  A W D R F T G T G D E E M A
  Q U W E R T Y H U A A A S S
  N A P I E R A S W N N M M U
  Z X V B N M K L O P U Y R S
```

DREAMS	PENDRAGON
JORDAN	PURSUE
MARLOW	ROMANCE
NAPIER	SEXY
NEW ZEALAND	SUSAN
OLIVIA	WINTER

Look for A YEAR DOWN UNDER Wordfind # 11
in November's Harlequin Presents # 1601
RELUCTANT CAPTIVE by Helen Bianchin. WF10

SOLUTIONS TO
WORDFIND # 10

YDU-OA